DOCTOR
Clause

USA TODAY BESTSELLING AUTHOR
C. A. KING

COVER DESIGNED BY THUNDERSTRUCK COVER DESIGNS

EDITOR:

KAREN HRDLICKA

FORMATTING BY: PARACOZE DESIGNS

This book is dedicated to all the romantics still waiting for their very own Doctor to appear and kiss everything better.

Also By C.A. King

Doctor D's Orderly Affair

Doctor Frank Enstein

Tropic Heat

Liberty

The Devil's Daughter

Curse of the Forbidden Island

Creatures of the Night

A Feather Out of Time

Shamrock & Clover

Clara's Story

High Heels & Mistletoe

Christmas Eve's Eve

Just Ducky

Freaky Finales

Twisted Tales of a Dead End Street

Strawberry Fields Dismembered

Grave Digger Academy

And more...

This book is a work of fiction. Any historical references, real places, real events, or real persons names and/or persona are used fictitiously. All other events, places, names and happenings are from the author's imagination and any similarities, whatsoever, with events both past and present, or persons living or dead, are purely coincidental.

Copyright © 2024 by C.A. King

ISBN: 979-8-3432393-6-2

All rights reserved. This book or any portion thereof may not be reproduced or used in any manner whatsoever without the express written permission of the author and/or publisher except for the use of brief quotations in a book review or scholarly journal.

Cover Design: Thunderstruck Cover Designs

Kings Toe Publishing

kingstoepublishing@gmail.com

Hamilton, Ontario. Canada

DR. CLAUSE

A doctor with a name crisis.
A mother with a child stuck in a hospital ward.
A way to raise money for kids for the holiday season.
A calendar in need of a December doctor.

Leeona isn't taking no for an answer. Her charity calendar needs one more hot doctor to agree to model, and quickly. Stephen Clause is smart and sexy—basically everything she's looking for. She'll do anything to convince him to sign on to the project.

Stephen has no interest in being Dr. December. There are already enough issues in his life stemming from the last name Clause without adding something else to the pile. The problem is, the feisty woman asking for a favour doesn't know when to give up.

The comment was meant as a joke and perhaps to embarrass her just enough to give up the ghost. He never expected her to agree to fulfill his entire naughty wish list in exchange for volunteering to pose as her sexy Santa.

CHAPTER ONE
STEPHEN

Owning a Jeep was a lifestyle choice; one which was only fully understood after the purchase was completed. The moment a person slid in the driver's seat, the call of the wild rushed through their veins, regardless of the location. Off road, in the city, it was all the same. Anywhere was the next safari, a jungle, or an unexpected expedition, despite whether it involved hours of driving, or just a twenty-minute jaunt to work.

With the top off, wind tousled hair, freeing the spirit. With it on, raging elements were no more than bugs squished on the windshield.

All terrain.

All weather.

All year round.

There were those who opted for a cherry-red sports car to fill a certain void in their lives. He opted for the same colour, but with the freedom of four-wheel drive.

Mid-life crisis be damned.

As a doctor, he knew: the feeling of adventure was enough to quell any of those symptoms before they reared their ugly heads.

Then there was the club which came complete with a secret handshake, so to speak. It was actually more of a wave, which consisted of two to four fingers extending upward from the steering wheel. Some thought the practise stemmed from soldiers returning from the war; the hand signal an acknowledgement of one another's service. The more modern version was much more simple; drivers offering a sign of respect to other Jeep lovers as they passed. Both were worthy explanations.

Sometime after that came the ducks.

The story behind the phenomena, which caught on like wildfire, began with one woman and a random act of kindness. She bought a bag of rubber ducks in a store and, out of goodwill, attached a small note to it which read, *Nice Jeep. Have a Great Day*, thereafter placing the duck in a door handle, where it waited to be discovered. When the little squeaker was found, the Jeep's owner immediately went to the same store as the woman, purchasing a bag of ducks of his own to pay-it-forward.

A few years later, Jeep dashboards everywhere were proudly sporting rubber ducks in every style and outfit imaginable.

Unfortunately, his ducks were all the same and a type he'd never put on display—Santa ducks. They came in every size and colour, but they all had one thing in common: each sported the red hat with a white trim and a pompom, known worldwide as the Christmas cap. There were variations, of course, some sported a knitted scarf, others sunglasses; there were tiny presents attached, stockings, bells, wreaths, poinsettias, the nice list, or the naughty list. If it had anything remotely to do with the holidays, he'd seen it in duck form.

If it ended at that, things would have been fine. But, it hadn't. There was more. Notes came with the bath toys he received, mostly from women, and all with a phone number, or an apartment number in his building, included.

Join me for some Christmas cheer.

DR. CLAUSE

I've been real naughty. Punish me.
Let me show you how good I can be.
You're what I really want under my tree.
Can I be your milk and cookies?
If I was the Grinch, I wouldn't steal Christmas, I'd steal you.
Have you ever done it in a sleigh?

I bet you have the stamina of a jolly, round man, capable of delivering joy all night long.

Keep an eye out for elves with ropes and a blindfold, because I'm asking for you this Christmas.

If it was a Christmas pickup line, he'd been ducked with it. Because of that, the second he saw or heard a cheesy come-on he bolted in the other direction, which was probably a major factor in the reason why he was still single. In fact, dating wasn't on the radar at all when the sleigh and tiny reindeer were.

Stephen hopped behind the wheel, tossing a handful of rubber duckies into a bin in the back seat. The moment Halloween was over, his dash and door handles filled with the things, and all because his last name was Clause and his first initial was S.

All his life there'd been torment over that name. No one cared the S stood for Stephen and not Santa. No one noticed the E on the end of Clause. People saw what they wanted to, especially when it came to the holidays. Because of that, the most wonderful time of the year was the absolute worst for him. There'd even been an occasion when he was bullied by classmates for not delivering the right presents, albeit, that took place during his childhood.

As an adult, people around him expected jolliness. That was difficult enough. Then there was the whole goodwill toward men thing. If there was a job which needed a volunteer, if there was a charity event needing a host, if there was a shift which needed covering, he was always the one looked to.

Bah Humbug!

This year he'd decided. If the S in his name wasn't standing for Stephen, it was going to be for Scrooge.

A quiet holiday was in the cards for once. No one was standing in his way.

CHAPTER TWO
LEEONA

A BALL OF YARN WAS THE EMBODIMENT OF RELAXATION. THE quality decided the feel of it. The better the yarn, the softer the texture. Likewise, the lower the calibre, the scratchier it felt against the skin. Both had their benefits. The only important detail about wool was making sure it was... well... woolly.

Natural fibre wasn't strictly for food anymore; it was growing in popularity for its therapeutic benefits. The repetitive nature of crafts involving needlework was akin to yoga and, in recent years, considered a form of meditation.

That's how the moms' knitting circle at Eastport General began—to alleviate the stress of having an ill child restricted to a hospital bed. They supported each other. They cried with one another. They made unique items to whittle away the hours together. If it could be knitted or crocheted, one of the moms was doing it.

The club also provided that wee bit of socializing necessary to remain sane, while providing an outlet to stay creative and productive. There were many uses for their creations too. Some were given to hospitalized children. Some were sold for charitable donations. Some were sold for profit.

For a single mom, with an ill or terminally ill child, a full-time job wasn't an option. Income mainly consisted of government handouts and charitable donations. Making handcrafted items was an alternative to welfare or in some cases boosted low incomes to more stable levels.

Of course, nothing was quite that easy. There needed to be an outlet from which to sell. Luckily, Leeona's sister was an indie jewellery crafter and willing to peddle both their wares at weekend markets.

"So," Menerva said in her usual nasal tone, "how are things coming along?"

"Fine," Leeona answered, raising the almost completed scarf in the air. That wasn't what the other woman was referring to though. She knew it, but wasn't looking forward to that conversation. Avoiding conflict like the plague was her motto.

"Pfft." Menerva arched one brow, while lowering the other slightly at the same time.

"Oh," Leeona sighed. "You meant the calendar. That's, well… you know. It still has a bit of a hiccup. I'm working on it though."

"Hiccup?" Menerva echoed. "It's more like projectile vomiting, if you ask me."

"It's not that bad," Leeona replied. "I'm just missing one doctor for the calendar. I'll find him. I just need a bit of time."

"Time?" Menerva echoed again. "How much time do you think you have? My cousin, Lenny, agreed to donate the photo shoot, and the printing costs, during the off-peak season. Now, it's the holiday rush, and you still have one month not booked."

"I know," Leeona said meekly. "We are all very grateful to you, and your cousin. The calendar wouldn't be possible without you both."

"Darn right," Menerva huffed. "Unfortunately, Lenny is on the verge of cancelling the whole thing." She shrugged. "He has to make a living, right?"

"He can't!" Leeona exclaimed. "We already have so many orders, and the children are counting on us to make their wishes come true for Christmas."

"He can!" Menerva bellowed back. "And he will. You have forty-eight hours to book a Dr. December or there won't be a charity calendar, and we will have to figure out funding another way."

A deadline, nothing was worse. At first, it seemed as if the job of finding the doctors to model was going to be easy-peasy, and it was for the first eleven. Eastport General was blessed with a plethora of handsome doctors willing to take one for the kids. After finding November, things took a turn for the worse. For some reason, the partners of some of the candidates for the final month were opposed to the idea of their men posing half-naked in photos, especially pictures the whole hospital, patients included, would inevitably see.

The simple solution was to have the doctor fully clothed, but eleven other shoots were already completed in a different style. Besides, December was an important month. People would be looking forward to it. The model needed to be special.

"Did you hear me?" Menerva scoffed.

"I did," Leeona piped up. "I'm meeting with a possible candidate this afternoon." That was a lie. "Oh. Look at the time. I better get moving."

"I think I speak for all the moms when I say; I expect to hear some positive news at our next get-together."

The weight of the room fell on her shoulders, making them droop. There was no candidate. There was no hope. The calendar was doomed. She was doomed.

Even the elevator was against her, stopping on every floor without need. No one was there when the doors opened and slowly closed again.

"Hello," Jordan said with an overly cheery smile. "How's everyone's favourite mom doing?"

That was the straw that broke the camel's back. The floodgate opened, tears pouring out. "I'm a horrible person," she sobbed. "I've let everyone down."

"Okay, honey," Jordan replied, rubbing her back. "Calm down. I am just going on break. How about we get a hot cup of tea and talk about it?"

Leeona nodded, sniffling. "Mmm."

CHAPTER THREE
STEPHEN

He was one of the lucky ones who actually had an office inside the hospital. That meant the door was either open or closed. Today it was closed.

He wasn't seeing any of the patients' family members, or taking any silly requests from peers. At least, that was the plan. Unfortunately, there was already a gift sitting on the desk when he arrived.

Air escaped his lips, lungs fully deflating.

It wasn't hard to guess what the gift was. The cute Christmas wrapping paper was a most unnecessary hint.

Every year it was the same.

The Santa suit.

It was always when the holidays approached. It always appeared in the same place. There was never a note. There was never a card. No one was willing to fess up to being the benefactor.

For some reason, his colleagues actually believed he was going to, one day, wear the outfit.

They were sadly mistaken.

That was never going to happen.

On the other hand, perhaps they simply enjoyed pushing his buttons, knowing the reaction their actions would bring about. He was easy prey.

With the parcel tucked neatly under one arm, he arrogantly dragged himself into the corridor, heading straight for the elevators. The lift doors immediately opened, as if they were afraid of getting in his way.

"Going down?" a female voice said.

The B button lit up.

This gift was going all the way to the bottom, the one floor no one enjoyed getting off on. In most cases, it was the end of the line. Whether the morgue or storage, there was an eerie air about the hallways. Frightening chills came with thoughts of what lay behind closed doors.

That one room was the same in every hospital, usually located on the lowest level—the store-it-all. It was barely ever entered, and what went in, never came out again. The items it housed were all well past their time, but still things which had been paid for by the hospital, and therefore, considered an asset.

Accounting departments were the biggest hoarders of all time.

He stepped over a box of decades-old decorations, first a string of knife-shaped tinsel cut outs, each dripping with dried-on, fake blood, from one Halloween or another. It was probably a surgical unit's idea of a prank, which undoubtedly wasn't well received.

Then came Christmas, some of which was more appropriate for a fright than goodwill, especially the frowning Santa with glowing green eyes.

In the end, it was all junk in need of a landfill, but simply tossing them away required too much paperwork. Red tape was everywhere, trying to trip him up.

A giant teddy, with a grim appearance, threatened to attack. If it fell on him, he was going down. The bear was the guardian of all things secret, all things, meaning a pile of years of red-and-white Santa suits. He tossed the latest version on the mound, watching it teeter for a moment, like a structure made from playing cards. He was an expert stacker though. It wasn't going to fall.

Palms brushed against one another.

That was it.

The terrifying bear was in charge now and he was rid of another silly costume meant to embarrass him. Sure, everyone else would get their jollies, snickering behind his back. It wasn't as gratifying for the one being made fun of though.

The venture into the hospital's museum of holidays past set him back. According to the time displayed on his phone's screen, the stash and dash took quite a bit longer than anticipated. That meant no trips outside the hospital for coffee or treats. The only other option was the cafeteria.

He probably shouldn't have left the lift. The moment the doors opened; he saw the crowd. Still, he strutted like a peacock into the thick of things, turning around immediately to walk pompously back out again.

It was that day; his least favourite of the week. Pots of coffee weren't even available. The kitchen staff had no time.

First, a new duck.

Then, a new red suit.

Now, no coffee.

It was one of those days.

The wrong buttons were exposed. If any were pushed, the results were going to be more grisly than the basement bear.

ROAR!

He could have pressed the open button and waited for another passenger. There was enough time, but then at what point would it stop. The lifts were always busy. Instead of acting in a courteous and polite manner, his gaze simply met with a woman's just as the crack between the doors became too small to ascertain any other details.

Her eyes were stunning though. The fact they caught his attention at all was proof of that.

CHAPTER FOUR
LEEONA

Tuesdays, for some reason, had the best menu of the week. At least, that seemed to be the general consensus. The cafeteria was packed from eleven in the morning, straight through to after the dinner rush.

Tex-Mex was popular. Besides the nacho bar, there were rice bowls, burritos, taco salad, chili, and a variety of side dishes.

"Here we go, sweetie," Jordan said, placing two piping hot cups of tea on the table between them. "So, tell me, what's going on, mama?"

"The calendar is in danger of being cancelled," she blurted out.

"No!" One hand covered his heart.

"Yes." Blowing on hot liquid wasn't cooling it down fast enough. A heaping helping of milk added to the brew. "I know you ordered several."

"I did," Jordan replied. "Why is it being cancelled?"

"Officially, it isn't, yet," Leeona admitted. "But I only have two days to find a doctor willing to model for the final month. Everyone either isn't interested, or their partners aren't willing to let them participate." She stood, palms slamming down on the table with force. "I need a single, hot doctor immediately!" An entire room of eyes turned in her direction.

"Don't we all, honey," Jordan laughed, taking the pressure off of her. "I need one of those, stat, too!" He nodded, whispering, "Sit and relax. Take a few deep breaths. You'll figure this out. Have a little faith in yourself."

"Wait! Who is that?" Leeona asked, glaring at a man in a white lab coat strutting through the cafeteria. "Is he a doctor?"

"Yes," Jordan answered.

"Is he single?"

"I believe so," Jordan replied.

"He's perfect!" she exclaimed.

"Oh no, honey," Jordan said, patting her hand. "You don't want to ask that doctor to play the role of the December hottie."

"Why not?" she asked. There was a check in every box, albeit most of the requirements were quite lax. The person needed to be a doctor, male, and hot.

Jordan leaned over the table. "He turns into a Scrooge when the holidays come around. Trust me, mama, he'd never accept."

"I still need to try," she said.

"I'm telling you," Jordan replied, "he's not going to agree to help. He can be quite harsh with folks who are trying to spread a bit of holiday cheer."

"I don't care," she huffed, standing her ground. "What's his name and where can I find him?"

"Dr. S. Clause," Jordan snickered.

"You're kidding."

"Nuh-uh." Jordan flashed a quirky smile. "That's his name. You can find him in the Oncology department. But I wouldn't go there, if I were you."

"Oh, I'm going," she insisted. "This is fate. Even his name is perfect. That man is going to be my December model, no matter what I need to do to make it happen."

"His name is the reason you shouldn't ask," Jordan said.

"I don't care," she insisted. "That man is going to be the calendar's December doctor."

Jordan glanced over at the man in question. "At least wait a day or two. He doesn't seem to be in a very good mood."

"I don't have a day, let alone two!" she exclaimed "I'm going." The tea splashed about in their cups, threatening to spill over the rims. Backs of chairs banged against one another. She was a woman on a mission; one who was able to match that doctor's strut, footstep for footstep.

If he was in a bad mood, she'd bring him out of it.

If he was being a Scrooge, she'd bring the ghosts of past, present and future.

If he said "no," she was going to make sure he took it back.

Too bad the elevator doors closed in her face before she had the chance to use all that courage and motivation. The ride up would have been a perfect opportunity to plead her case. Now, the doctor had home-court advantage.

CHAPTER FIVE
STEPHEN

Tap. Tap.

It was faint—faint enough to be ignored.

Knock.

Knock.

It was also annoying and growing louder.

"Come in!" He glanced up, instantly recognizing the woman as the one he'd left back on the main floor.

"Hi." She inched forward, wringing the straps on a black purse. Just a bit tighter and they might have snapped right through. "I'm Leeona."

"Well, Leeona, what can I do for you?" he asked, unsure as to why the woman was bothering him. There were no appointments on his calendar and no messages as to a new patient.

"I represent a group of mothers raising money for the children who will be stuck in the hospital for the holidays," she said.

The drawer opened; a chequebook appearing on the desk. "How much?" A donation was manageable, if it meant the woman left.

"Oh, no," Leeona chuckled. "Well, I suppose it couldn't hurt. I mean to say; I wouldn't turn down a contribution to the cause, but that's not exactly what I came to see you about."

Scratching.

Rustling.

Ripping.

The filled-in cheque slid across the desk, coming to stop at the very edge closest to her. Rather than taking a few steps, she went up on tiptoes, stretching her neck out to see the amount written on it.

Gasp! "Wow!" she finally said. "That's very generous of you, Doctor..." She glanced once more in a similar fashion. "Clause? S. Clause?" A schoolgirl chuckle escaped slightly parted lips. Jordan was telling the truth. "That actually makes things much easier."

His eyes narrowed to thin slits. "What does?" He already knew the woman expected something from him, on account of his name being similar to that of the jolly old man.

"I'm." She paused. "The mother's club is putting together a calendar for charity."

"No!" he exclaimed loudly.

"I haven't finished yet," Leeona complained. "We already have the photographer and publisher in place, not to mention the fact that eleven other doctors have already signed on to the project and had their shoots."

"No!" he replied a bit louder.

"We only need one more doctor," she continued, ignoring his protests. "You would be a perfect fit for Dr. December."

"No!" he bellowed. This woman was the attractive but annoying type—the sort who rarely took a reply of any sort at face value.

"Why not?" she asked. "Do you actually have a valid reason?"

"I don't need a reason," he complained. "I have the right to refuse being photographed half-naked for the whole hospital to see."

"So, you are shy?" she asked. "Hmm. We can make sure you are represented in a dignified manner." Fingers snapped, her eyes lighting up. "A Santa suit would be perfect."

"Absolutely not," he raged.

"I don't understand," she said, shoulders and mood somewhat deflated. "Even your name is perfect for the part."

"That's precisely why I don't want to," he answered.

"Do you have a girlfriend?" Leeona said, once again ignoring his words. "Is she the reason you won't help us?"

"No," he sighed. "I'm single."

"You don't like children?"

Time in an already packed schedule was ticking by and this woman wasn't leaving. Short of throwing her out, there was little to be done.

Or was there?

"Please." Her hands folded together, making a sign of prayer.

"You know what? Sure," he chuckled. "Why not?"

"Really?" Her eyes widened with anticipation. "Truly? You want to fill the spot?"

"No!" A book slammed down on his desk. "I'm not interested in being your Dr. December... but I will."

Jumping for joy, her hands came together, clapping loudly. "Oh! Thank you."

"Wait!" he bellowed. "I will pose for the calendar, if you agree to fulfill every wish on my naughty list."

"Deal!" With that she was gone.

"Huh?" His jaw dropped.

It worked in a sense. The woman left, but he never expected her to agree to the terms. Was she really planning on acting out a stranger's fantasies so easily? There was a huge morality issue for both of them to consider.

Captivation?

Fascination?

Whatever the case, she'd caught his attention enough to

make him shift positions. Two fingers pulled on the collar of his button-down shirt, fingers lightly caressing his neck. Work wasn't going to get finished easily; he was completely stiff.

CHAPTER SIX
LEEONA

One hand covered her chest, keeping her heart from beating right out of it. She slid to the floor, back against a wall.

What just happened?

It was spur-of-the-moment.

It was completely out of character.

It was totally insane.

Sure, she had a Dr. December now, but at what cost? Her body was up for grabs. Who knew what he was going to do to her? Who knew what the man's fantasies entailed?

Teeth grated over her bottom lip, biting down harder at the edge.

Who knew what any man's fantasies were? She certainly wasn't an expert in that department. There was a distinct lack of experience in her portfolio.

There'd only been one guy in her life, and he wasn't exactly the pinnacle of erotica. In fact, when they did the nasty, he was usually drunk. There was never any adventure. There was never any attempt at trying new things.

Wham. Bam. Thank you, ma'am.

It was done. It was over. He fell asleep, snoring. She'd never even climaxed—not once. Some women weren't able to. She'd always assumed she fit into that category. Not that it mattered. Her son, Tommy, was the most important thing in her life. Miles hit the road running the moment their son was diagnosed with a possibly terminal disease.

What was she thinking?

There was no way she could go through with this. What if other people found out? What if the other moms found out? What if her son found out?

It was scandalous.

Mixed emotions made her more aware of her own self. So much was going on. It was exciting. It was thrilling. At the same time, there was a building anxiety, and of course a touch of anticipation. It certainly wasn't in any way boring. Maybe that was what she was looking for; a way to fill a monochrome world with a bit of colour.

A light blush filled her cheeks, the warmth drawing her hands, and the gentle caress of fingers skating around in circular motions.

That smouldering gaze.

He'd mesmerized her in a way no one ever had before.

Poor choices were made over less. Miles was a prime example. She was still a virgin when they tied the knot. Their wedding night was the first time a man touched her, not that there'd been much of that. The deed was over before she knew what was happening. That was normal though. Men ejaculated quickly. Two minutes was all it took.

"Ohh!"

Her head shook, hands both planted on either side. Regardless of a stiffening posture, there was a bad case of ants in the pants to deal with.

The need to find a final doctor for the calendar was a factor, but it wasn't the whole reason for agreeing to his terms. She wasn't even sure what was, but in the moment he asked—she wanted to say yes—she wanted to agree to anything Dr. S. Clause desired—she wanted to be on the naughty list, and maybe even punished for it.

These sensations were all new, especially the tingling feeling between her thighs. Her body wanted something, but she wasn't quite sure what.

"Find out," she mumbled under her breath. "I need to know."

Eyes veered from one side to the other, searching for anyone who might have seen her in such a state. Her thoughts, no doubt, were readable. Her body language gave everything away. She was raring to go and, given the chance, might have jumped the doctor right then and there.

"Ha!"

That was yet another first. She'd never instigated sex before. There'd never been the need—or the desire.

A silly grin crossed her lips.

Everyone in the moms' club took on a job in connection with the charity calendar. She was certainly glad she'd been the one chosen to find the models.

CHAPTER SEVEN
STEPHEN

SunSleep, one of the largest hotels in Eastport, was almost directly across the street from the hospital, less than a five-minute walk, in fact. That made it ideal for doctors scheduled with late nights and early mornings, as well as patients waiting for procedures and their families.

A suite was perfect. The living area meant there was no one needed to enter the bedroom. Plans were on the verge of erotic, but there was no need for touching, at least until he wrapped his head around the morality of the situation.

Watching was another thing. If a woman wanted to be an exhibitionist in front of him, who was he to stop her? If she bolted at the thought, problem solved.

He glanced at his wrist. It was still early. There was enough time. The bathroom was a work of art, including the multi-heads, each with their own handle. One turned under the force of a tight grip. Imitation raindrops fell from a square panel in the ceiling. A single finger extended, testing the spray.

Cold.

Warm.

Just right.

Clothes landed in a pile on the tile floor. One foot stepped onto the non-slip surface, the other following close behind. Typically, he indulged in two showers a day. One, to start the day off refreshed, and the other to wind down.

This was exactly what was needed after a long and troublesome day. The stress removing ability of a rain shower was no joke. It was calming, therapeutic, and cleansing. What more was there, apart from knowing a pair of silk pyjamas was waiting when he was done? The effects of the material's delicate softness were equally mellowing.

Relaxing was a vital part of the decompression process. Feeling good about himself was equally as important.

Knock.

He left the buttons on the top undone, answering the door. There was only one possible person on the other side.

She actually showed up.

A part of him, the more intelligent part, hoped she wouldn't. The bulge in his pants, however, was happy to see her.

"Come in," he said, towel-drying his hair. He plopped down on the couch, watching her flailing about in a most unusual manner. "Find a spot and stay there."

She nodded, teeth biting her bottom lip. "Like this?" Feet pointed out, positioned slightly away from each other, and posture straight, for the most part.

"Sure." A controller clicked, dimming the lights, and turning on an explicit movie in the background, which only he had a view of.

Minutes passed before the weight of staying still set in. Her body teetered, swaying. "Is this it? Your fantasy is to watch a porno while I do nothing?"

"Not exactly," he replied. "Among other things, I like to watch. This is just the beginning. Are you that eager to enact all of my desires? You don't even know what they entail."

"Well," she said, still standing in the middle of the room. "I feel rather awkward at the moment. So, please tell me. What would you like me to do?"

He felt the stupid grin crossing his face, but there was no stopping it. "Undress," he replied, legs sprawling wide open.

"Sorry?" she answered, clearing her throat right after. A light pink blush filled her cheeks.

"Undress," he repeated. "You asked me to tell you what I want you to do. I want you to take your clothes off."

"Right here?" she asked.

"Right there," he answered, eyes glued to her. If she ran, it was over. If she stayed, it would be a good show. Either way, he wasn't breaking any rules in the ethics department.

"Everything?" she asked.

"Everything." The ice cubes in his cup clanged together, swirling amongst an amber-coloured liquid. He took a small sip. "I want to see you strip."

"Strip." She gulped back. "I'm not a spring chicken anymore. I've had a child. Things aren't in the same place as they were when I was in my early twenties."

"I'm a doctor," he snickered. "I think I know a thing or two about what happens to the body during the aging process." This woman had no self-confidence. Why? It made no sense. She was attractive with her clothes on and he was pretty sure without them would be just as pleasant to the eye. "Go on then." Curiosity had the best of him as to where she'd start.

The shoes?

It was all he could do to avoid laughing, watching the medium-height woman hopping around on one foot while she pulled off each shoe. That display was followed by socks.

"Phew." She straightened up. "That was a chore, wasn't it?"

That part she wasn't embarrassed by for some reason. It was more a disappointing commotion than a sexy show. The pants were pretty much the same, legs tripping over one another. She barely stayed upright. This woman was definitely going through with the request and in a most amusing manner.

The buttons on her blouse undid easily, it fell to the floor in the pile with everything else. That left what was under the top layers: granny underwear.

She was mesmerizing, his type exactly, yet put zero effort into her own sexiness.

Her confidence levels registered well below par.

There could be only one reason why; she'd never been treated right.

"Keep going," he urged, taking note of every curve and dimple she had to offer.

Some men never understood the beauty of a voluptuous woman. He'd always enjoyed having a bit extra to hold on to. Skin and bones were basically the same as looking at a medical skeleton. That certainly wasn't a turn-on. Leeona, despite her lack of seductive garments, already had his dick twitching.

Without a stitch of clothing left, it was easy to deduce two things. One, there were no tan lines. Most of her time was spent indoors. Two, she lacked pride in her own appearance and self-worth.

There was a lot to be learned about a person from how they handled their own nudity. Embarrassment was a self-conscious emotion. All doctors knew that. She had a bad case of it, wiggling about, unable to allow her arms to simply fall at her sides. Still, there was an attractiveness to that as well.

One hand reached inside his silk lounger.

"Shouldn't I be doing that?" she asked.

"Why?" he replied with a question of his own. "Were you hoping I'd make tonight about you... make you scream between the sheets?"

"No," Leeona gasped. "That's not what I was thinking, I swear. I mean I can't anyway." She snorted a nervous laugh.

"Can't what?" he asked, his hand returning to the opening.

"I am one of those women... you know... who can't climax," she explained.

"Who told you that?" he asked. "It's absolutely not true. There may be a small percentage of women who find it hard to orgasm during the actual act of intercourse, but I assure you, you can come. I'll prove it to you."

"How?" she asked.

"Touch yourself," he instructed.

"Do what?!" she exclaimed.

"Start with the breasts," he continued. "Circle around the nipple lightly, until it forms an erect peak. Then flick it, massage it, find what feels good."

Leeona wet her lips, following the directive to a T.

"If it feels good, moan," he said.

"Mmm."

"Good." He sat up straight. "Is the heat growing between your legs?"

She simply nodded; eyes closed.

"Are you wet?" he asked. "Move your fingers between your legs."

"Wouldn't it be better if someone else was doing this?" she asked, still gently twisting the sensitive parts of her own breasts.

"You need to understand your own body," he answered. "You can't share a moment like this with a partner, if you don't know what it is you enjoy. Figuring out your own sexual preferences is the key to climaxing."

She nodded, allowing a finger to probe between her legs.

"That's it," he said, leaning back again to fulfill his own growing needs. "Slide the fingers back and forth. Allow them to enter you, then draw them slowly back out. Feel around for any spots you enjoy feeling touched, then concentrate on them. Increase the speed and pressure of the rubbing." His own hand moved up and down on his shaft in pace with her timing.

"Oh!" she cried out, her body trembling.

He'd finished a moment earlier, giving him just enough time to catch her before both legs buckled beneath her. Heavy breaths gave way to a light snore. The first orgasm was always one for the books. It certainly caught the woman in his arms off guard and drew out all that was wearisome, allowing for a deep slumber.

Maybe sex wasn't such a bad idea, after all.

Next time.

CHAPTER EIGHT
STEPHEN

SHE WAS ALL THAT FILLED HIS MIND: THE CURVE OF HER HIPS, THE perkiness of her breasts, the slight blush on her cheeks.

Being seduced by feminine wiles was something he'd managed to avoid up until then. So, why now? Why her? Sure, she was attractive, but there'd been other beautiful women chasing him.

Was Leeona chasing him, or vice versa?

The answer was rather obvious, considering he was the one standing outside a lingerie shop, peeking in. The sales person inside was going to take him for a pervert, if he didn't go in soon.

Granny undies had their place, but that wasn't anywhere near the bedroom. Feeling attractive was something everyone needed. Clothing, especially underwear and sleep attire, played an important role in that.

Comfort, quality, and beauty were all things the right intimate wear had to offer a man or woman.

Those were all the things she needed to feel. That's what he was looking for.

Ding.

A bell on the door alerted the salesperson he was there.

"Hello," she said in an overly joyful tone. "How can I help you today?"

An overwhelming floral scent wafted about. It might have been satchels of potpourri, a special air freshener, or a staggeringly strong perfume. Whatever the case, it was too strong. Anyone with a sensitive nose was bound to have problems there. Even he wanted to spend as little time as possible shopping.

These stores were overlooking the obvious. The human body produced tiny chemicals which gave off a special scent. Pheromones added to intimate experiences and communicated sexual arousal between partners. Covering them up was a crime.

"I'm looking to buy a certain woman a few things," he said, frowning at the roughness of the material of some underwear in a bin.

"Your wife?" the woman asked. "Girlfriend? Do you know her size?" She passed him a small questionnaire sheet to fill in.

"Mmm," he grunted. There'd been plenty of competitions with classmates in medical school which revolved around guessing female measurements. He'd won every time. That practice wasn't lost to him.

"Great!" the salesperson exclaimed, looking over the jotted down notes. "Let me show you a few popular pieces."

"Okay." He took a seat on a bench in front of the changing rooms, waiting for her return. How many men sat there, biding their time before a dirty little fashion show began, their wives and girlfriends the models? Modesty had no place when it came to sexual pleasure.

"This plus-sized baby-doll comes with a matching G-string and has adjustable straps for comfort," the saleswoman suggested, strutting about as if she were the one modelling it and not the hanger.

From the material it was obvious, it was a little too constrictive. There was no flow, allowing it to gracefully drape a body.

"Hmm." He shook his head. "I'm not sure it would do her justice."

"If you are looking for something more vibrant, we have a similar garment in a fiery-red colour." The woman was a professional, carefully watching his body movements for an opportunity to seal the deal. Her paycheques were, no doubt, commission-based.

"What about something in a silk chiffon?" he asked.

The woman's brows arched. "You know your stuff." She fired off a wink. "Regular chiffon is a bit rough and can cause irritation. The silkier version of the material glides gently against the skin. It's a bit more difficult to care for though. If that's a problem, I suggest forgetting chiffon altogether and just choosing something in silk."

He nodded. That made sense. "And I'd like to see a few lacy items." There was no doubt he was purchasing at least one outfit in that material. "Also, can you bring out a few things which have a peekaboo design?" That was something he'd come to cherish back in his college days, and was definitely on the list.

The trip started out as a way of helping to build her self-confidence. Of course, there was no reason why his own preferences weren't to be taken into consideration at the same time.

Several more skimpy outfits joined the fray on display. Deciding on just a few was difficult. Each of the saleswoman's offerings had its own unique appeal. There were other items to be considered as well, including regular bra and panty sets.

He'd only meant to get a few things, but walked out with three bags worth of skivvies and a couple nighties.

After all that, there were some high expectations about the

coming evening's activities. Of course, there was no pressure on her, despite his growing desire. He was happy to keep watching her. The next time they met in private, she was going to feel good about herself, if nothing else.

CHAPTER NINE
LEEONA

NOTHING WAS WIPING THE SMILE FROM HER FACE. THE BREEZE freezing it in place had already blown sometime during the night. Now, she was stuck with it, no matter how dire the circumstances around her were.

"Are you taking this seriously?" her sister, Pina, asked.

A light brown liquid poured from a clear pot, fragrant flowers remaining trapped inside. Those types of teapots were all the rage a few years back, having been designed to allow tea-lovers a full range of enjoyment, spanning across all the senses.

The visuals of the blooming flowers.

The fragrant scent of the buds.

The light floral taste.

One needed to be a real tea enthusiast to fully understand the appeal. That's why the whole craze died down. It was simply a novelty item to the average loose-leaf drinker.

"What is the plan?"

That was an odd question coming from her closest relative. "I don't know." There was never a plan. There was never an emergency fund. Living by the seat of her pants, not knowing where the money was coming from was the norm.

"Well, it can't stay here," Pina complained. "It's blocking me in."

"I don't have a spot to take it to," she complained. "You know I don't. I need a bit of time, maybe a few days, to figure out how I am going to pay to have it fixed."

"Fine." Pina shook her head. "I'll get my neighbours to help me push it onto the street when they get home. You can't leave it longer than two days though."

"I can't go without a car for longer than that," she snorted. "Hopefully, it is just something small this time."

"It's old," Pina said. "It's time to think about getting something more reliable. Maybe you can lease a newer vehicle."

"Pfft." One hand waved her sister off. "I can't afford an extra dime on my budget. A new car, even a used one, is out of the question. You know that."

"Hmm?" Pina eyed her up and down. "You are taking this awfully well. Usually, you'd have broken down in tears three or four times by now. So spill it! What's with the grin?" She gasped. "Are you seeing someone?"

There was no hiding anything from a sister. "Maybe." She shrugged.

"Who is he?" her sister pried. "What does he look like? Where did you meet him? What does he do? Tell me everything."

"Whoa." Her white mug pushed across the counter for a refill. "That's a lot of questions all at once. I met him at the hospital. He's a doctor."

"A doctor, huh?" Pina chuckled. "He has money then. Why not ask him to help you out?"

"I can't do that!" she exclaimed. "We've only been out one time."

"And you are sleeping with him?" Pina chuckled, brows waggling suggestively. "I never pegged you for a sex on the first date sort of gal."

"I'm not!" she insisted. "I mean, we haven't."

"Your ear-to-ear grin says otherwise," Pina replied, taking a long sip of tea, while still eyeing her sister carefully. "I've never seen you so laid-back and relaxed. You... had an orgasm."

"Huh?!" She drew in a breath of air, filling her lungs to capacity. "Maybe I did. But that doesn't mean we went all the way. In fact, he never touched me."

"What? How does that work?"

"Well," she said, shifting her bottom on the stool. "I wanted to. I mean, I really wanted to. He said he wasn't ready. So..." Teeth grated over her bottom lip.

"So?" her sister asked. "Don't leave me hanging."

"I did it myself," she said in a tone just above a whisper.

"You?!" her sister exclaimed. "My sister?! The biggest prude I know, masturbated?! What brought on this change? Don't get me wrong, it's nice to see you a little more serene, but it's not really in your nature."

She shrugged. "Deep down, I think I wanted a change. I missed out on so much with Miles. And then..."

"And then a doctor's diagnosis came in?" Pina chuckled.

"Mm-hmm." Her grin expanded, tugging her skin tight. "He said I needed to understand myself before I could expect someone else to."

"Ooo." Pina fanned her face. "I like this man. When do I get to meet him?"

"I don't know," she answered. "Like I said, it's only been one night." The part about the deal was conveniently left out of the conversation. There was a chance what she was doing with the good doctor wasn't necessarily classified as a date and never would be. "Whatever will be, will be."

"Mom used to say that," Pina mused. "You know, I'm glad you found something just for you."

CHAPTER TEN
STEPHEN

She was nowhere to be found—not in his office—not in the cafeteria. Where else would she be? Sadly, that was almost the full extent of his knowledge of her. They hadn't even exchanged contact information.

The moms' club!

She was a member. Maybe that's where she was hiding. Too bad that was on the one floor he never visited: the pediatric ward.

It wasn't that he disliked children. They were like other people, only smaller. It was the questions they came up with which were brutal, plus, during the most magical time of the year, they had a tendency to ask for things he wasn't able to give.

They wanted to go home for the holidays.

They wanted to play with other kids.

They wanted to go to school.

They wanted all the things healthy children took for granted.

He was just a regular doctor. Those things were well out of his reach. No red sack contained magical cures. If it were possible, he would have happily spread that sort of cheer on every floor and then some. It wasn't though. That's why he never visited the children's wing. That's why he only treated adults. While still sad, losing someone who'd already lived a full life was easier than watching youth lose their battles, day after day.

Abandoning his own rules, he was already there, moving swiftly through the corridor to the waiting area. A set of double doors pulled open.

"Leeona?"

The room fell silent, a half-dozen sets of curious eyes glaring back at him. Most were probably wondering what his relationship with Leeona was. There were also a few slowly undressing him. The difference between the two types of leers was obvious.

"She's not here," one woman stated firmly. "We haven't seen her all morning. Might I ask, are you the newest calendar doctor?"

He nodded. "Do you know where I can find her?"

"Have you tried her son's room?" another woman suggested. "She spends a lot of time there. It's to be expected, of course."

"Thank you," he replied, backing out rather than turning around. Part of him was quite leery about the group, which was intensely eyeing him up and down. There was even a bit of drool action happening. His butt certainly wasn't there for their amusement. Smacking or pinching was strictly prohibited, at least by that group. For Leeona, allowances could be made.

Ever since he joined the staff at Eastport General, there'd been plenty of cougars chasing him. One elderly group in particular, staying at the SunSleep, actually mistook him for a role-playing stripper. Once grandma latched on, she wasn't letting go. That night was going to haunt the corridors of the hotel until the end of days as their biggest scandal. It took four large security guards, and a call to the local police, to clear up the misunderstanding. The mishap ended all future group discount rates, hen parties, and stag-and-doe events on the property.

Dirty old ladies aside, he wasn't opposed to nakedness. Looking at another human form was a healthy part of life. Being aroused by an attractive body was a normal response. Touching without permission was a totally different situation. There lay his dilemma with Leeona. She'd consented, but to what? He wasn't sure she even knew. Until she directly asked him for his involvement, it was hands-off.

"Look don't touch," he mused, arriving at his destination.

Leeona's son's room was easy enough to find. In fact, he'd already located it during the long walk to the moms' support team at the very end of the corridor.

Despite being semi-private, there was only one bed occupied. That wasn't uncommon for any cancer ward. It was a brutal disease, which resulted in a large turnover of patients. One day there'd be a neighbour to chat with, the next an empty bed with new sheets. Sometimes there wasn't even enough time for neighbours to exchange names.

"Hi," he gleefully said, entering as if he were visiting one of his own patients. "How are you today?" Instantly, the visit became less about Leeona and more about her son. Maybe it was the child's appearance; the delicate skin under his eyes unnaturally darkened, sunken, and hollow. That was the only colour to be found on an otherwise pale complexion.

"Who are you?" the boy replied, face expressionless. "A new doctor? No one mentioned anything about seeing someone new."

"You're Tommy, right?"

The thin child nodded slowly, without saying a word.

"I'm a friend of your mom's," he said, pulling up a chair. The physician in him glanced over at a chart hanging on the end of the bed. It wasn't his place to look though. He had no right to interfere. "Has she been in today?"

"No." Chapped lips pursed together. "She was supposed to be here a while ago." He shrugged. "Something probably happened."

"Like what?" he asked.

"I dunno," the boy snapped. "Maybe the car broke down again. Maybe she got a speeding ticket. Maybe she just got caught up in some charity work." He went back to staring out the window at nothing in particular.

"You're pretty calm for your age," he said.

"Not really," Tommy sighed. "I'm just bored. There's nothing to do here but wait for the next dose of medicine. The meals aren't even worth looking forward to. I hate food now. I used to love my mom's cooking."

"She's a good cook?" Stephen asked.

His head slowly nodded, expression remaining blank. "From what I remember." He paused, heaving a sigh. "It all tastes like cardboard now."

His thumb jutted out, pointing toward the door. "Do you want me to grab you a book or maybe get you a puzzle?"

"Nah," Tommy replied. "I've read them all, and the puzzles are missing pieces."

"Oh." Once again hospital protocols of not throwing anything away were in full play. "What about a toy?"

"There aren't any," Tommy answered. "Unless you count the waiting room ones. I don't. Most of them are broken, or for really small kids."

"Right." He never considered what it meant to be a child stuck in Eastport General before. The hospital prioritized medical needs over books, toys, artwork, and even magazines. It never crossed his mind or anyone else's, other than the moms' club, how dull that was."

For adults, there was no need to provide activities. They came, waited, had their appointments and, for the most part, left. Those who needed extended stays owned smartphones or tablets to pass the time when they weren't resting.

"Can I get you a magazine from the shop in the lobby?" he suggested, thumb sticking out, pointing toward the door.

"No," Tommy replied. "I'd just flip through it and then toss it. It's not worth wasting money. If you want to do something for me, do it for everyone. We are all on the same journey, going to the same destination, and taking the same boring route getting there."

Tommy was beyond his years in wisdom.

He glanced over the boy once more. "It was nice to meet you, Tommy. I hope we can talk again some time."

"You!" Jordan exclaimed from the doorway, before strutting in like a runway model. "What are you doing here? Where is Leeona?"

"I don't know," Stephen said, pointing. "But you are just the person I wanted to see."

Jordan's newly pencilled-on eyebrows arched. "I am?"

"You are," he replied. "Come with me."

"Ha-ha," Jordan chuckled. "I thought you'd never ask." He walked quickly, taking small steps while keeping up to the doctor leading the way. "Where, exactly, are we going?"

"To the parking garage." Hands folded together after pushing the button for sub-level one. "This way." One hand motioned for the orderly to exit the elevator first.

"This is all so sudden," Jordan said. "I wasn't expecting this sort of invitation. Are you sure I'm the one you need?"

"Quite," he replied. The back hatch of his Jeep opened, both arms reaching in. "Here. What do you think?"

"Ducks?" Jordan said. "They are adorable, but I'm not sure why you are giving them to me. Roses might be a better touch."

"What would kids do with roses?" he snapped.

"Oh. Ohh." Jordan's mouth remained open. "You want to give

these to the kids to play with. I get you." He nodded, cracking a half-smile. "S. Clause to the rescue."

"It's not like that," he huffed. "I was going to toss these out anyway. I just figured, before going to the landfill, maybe someone else could make use of them." He glanced away. "Do you think the kids would want them?"

"Heck yeah," Jordan answered. "They will love them. Believe it or not, their wish lists are pretty tame. Trust me, I've seen them. Anything will bring a smile to those little faces." The box juggled in his arms. "You're okay, Dr. Clause." The box lifted. "I'll go drop these off at the nurses' station."

"Thanks," he mumbled. "I have work to do."

And a certain mom to find.

CHAPTER ELEVEN
STEPHEN

Not a single word. He never heard hide nor hair from her for the entire day and he'd been waiting so patiently.

Maybe the deal was off, if that was possible at this point. He'd already watched quite the show. But he hadn't touched her, yet. The part of him twitching in his pants wasn't content with leaving things like that. He wanted her. There was no doubt about it. What started out as a joke was now the very fantasy he'd been deep down inside hoping for.

Still, there were so many morally grey areas involved in this relationship.

He paused briefly at the hotel's main entrance before heading in.

Was this a relationship? If not, what was it? How long would it continue? How far would they go? After the photos were taken, was she going to dump him?

One foot tapped on the tiled floor. A prickly sensation ran up his spine. What if she was there? His heart hammered in his chest. What if she wasn't?

There was only one way to find out.

Ding.

The elevator ride was longer than he remembered it being. Anticipation flip-flopped between a sense of urgency and one of pure dread. Not knowing was slowly eating away at him. The moment the ride was finished, there was a mad dash to the suite, stopping only for a moment to catch his breath before entering.

"You're here," he said, cracking a smile.

"I am," she replied, standing in the same spot from the previous evening, this time wearing one of the lacy outfits he'd left on the coffee table. "I assumed this was for me."

"You assumed correctly," he said. "Where were you today?"

"I had some errands to run," she replied. "And my car broke down. Things became unhinged a bit after that."

"You should have called," he said, pulling off his tie. "I might have been able to help."

"I don't have your number." A slight grin formed in the corners of her lips. "I didn't want to use the hospital line. That's for your work."

"I am allowed personal calls too," he argued. "Especially emergency ones." What was done, was done. There was no point in pushing the idea of asking for help after the fact. Hopefully, next time, if there was one, she would. "That looks lovely on you."

"I've never worn anything like this before," she said, shifting weight between her legs. "I never thought about lingerie."

"And?" The buttons on his shirt were already undone, the front open. "How does it feel?"

"Good," she admitted, her nipples stiffening under the material, almost threatening to poke through. "I'm starting to realize the value of spending a bit of money on a few pretty things like this. How much do I owe you?"

He waved her off. "It's a gift. They all are."

"But why?"

"It's all part of setting the stage," he explained. "A sexual experience is heightened by knowing what we want and making it happen. Part of that is our choice in outfits. Think of how you want to feel... how you want your partner to feel... what would make achieving those desires easiest."

"That's all?" she asked.

"Seeing you like this benefits me, as well," he said, a sly smile forming in the corners of his lips. "I can instantly spot how that outfit makes you feel. Erogenous zones can become quite sensitive, just grazing one of those areas can be stimulating. The tightness of lace against your nipples is turning you on, without me doing a thing."

"Ah!" she groaned. "But they want more. They want your touch."

He moved closer, hands lightly caressing her waist, bottom, back. Teasing, but not fulfilling her request.

"Please!" she begged. "Please, show me everything. I want you to teach me."

"Teach," he echoed. That in itself was a fantasy. To have an attractive woman asking him to show her what pleasure was all about was a dream come true. From that moment forward, there was no holding back.

He swiftly moved to face her, breath matching breath, heartbeat matching heartbeat. Memories of his first kiss flooded back with the taste of her candy-floss-flavoured lip gloss. He was a teen again, but this time with experience under his belt. This wasn't a sloppy kiss, wet yes, but messy no. It was a well-crafted sensual experience—lesson number one—show don't tell.

The tip of his tongue gently stroked her lips, before pushing its way inside to tickle the roof of her mouth.

Lesson number two was in tongue play. The two intertwined, sharing a dance similar to a musicless version of the tango. When the final dip was over, it was time for a bit of sucking and a light nibble or two.

"Mmm," she moaned, breathless from their kisses. "Please," she begged again. "Show me more."

There was no refusing such a passionate request. Still, at the back of his mind, the dreaded shoot awaited.

Leeona was living up to all his expectations, there was no way of reneging on the deal after the fact. The only problem was, a calendar, albeit only useful for one year, was forever. If nothing was done, their play dates were coming to an end.

CHAPTER TWELVE
LEEONA

THE FEELING OF FACING THE UNKNOWN, OF TRYING SOMETHING for the first time was a thrill—a pure shot of adrenaline administered directly into the bloodstream.

Her breath was hot and heavy.

Her chest was beating faster than ever.

She'd already learned so much. There were mega-sensitive areas of the body that were quick to respond to the touch.

The neck.

The mouth.

The tongue.

The lips.

Nipples.

The entire area between her legs.

That was only the beginning of the list. There were many places which hadn't even been tested yet. A deep curiosity about sexual sensations was growing within her. The blindfold she wore, up until that point, had been ripped off and a lifetime of unfulfilled needs were finally being met. A doorway leading to new pleasures swung wide open and nothing was going to shut it again.

This wasn't about escaping reality. It was making what was real better.

His tongue on her lips, in her mouth, turned every part of her body into an erogenous zone. The taste wasn't enough to satisfy. It wasn't the full seven-course meal she wanted. For that, she needed to order the works.

"Please!" she begged, panting. "I want to feel you touching me." The stage was set. There was no going back, not that she wanted to.

His hands were on her, gently teasing their way across less sensitive spots, mocking the ones crying out for attention. The roughness of the lace scratched against delicate bits.

Pain.

Pleasure.

The lines blurred between the two.

His fingers were gentle. The caress was light.

Nipples stood at attention; the material of her undergarment causing extreme friction. There was no padding in this particular ensemble to take the edge off.

The push.

The pull.

It all made her even more aware of his finger circling her breasts, searching out small holes in the fabric and slowly making them bigger.

Rip!

The tip of one tit was freed. The other remained a prisoner.

The second kiss was as delightful as the first; his mouth surrounding the newly exposed area of her breast.

Tongue flicked.

Lips sucked.

Every nerve in her body stood at attention, awaiting further instruction. He was her teacher, her lover, and so much more.

"Do you like that?" he asked, bedroom eyes glistening in the dimmed light. "It's important for you to tell me if you enjoy what I am doing, or if it is too much."

"Shut up," she demanded. "Keep going." She was on the verge of climax from just nipple play, something she never believed possible before. The lace top lifted, kisses lining her midsection as she finished removing the top.

"You taste delightful," he said, warm breath tickling exposed skin. "I could devour you all night long." He paused, playfully staring into her eyes as he took a nipple in his mouth, tongue gently rolling over and around before coming up for air again. This time he pushed her breasts together, sucking on both at the same time, sensitive tips rubbing against one another as well as having the sensation of his fluttering tongue.

"Oh!" she moaned, her body stiffening, desperately trying to rub against him.

"Not yet," he said in a deep gruff voice. "Come for me."

Thighs rubbed together. The bottom part of her still had the lace panties to take full advantage of, moving back and forth, pressing against the material.

"Yes!" she screamed, body stiffening, before releasing a tidal wave, leaving her dripping wet. This one was even more intense than the one brought about by masturbation.

"Careful," he said, catching her just as wobbly knees buckled. "Let's take this in the other room." He chuckled softly. "You may need to lie down for the next part."

"Next part?" she huffed, still breathless. "There's more?"

"Much." He fired off a playful wink. "We are only just beginning."

Love-making sessions that lasted for hours were tall tales made up by men lacking confidence, at least that was what she always believed. Even in his arms, heading for the bedroom, it was hard to imagine. Her body was on a full stimulation overload. Even the slightest graze was too much to handle.

"Don't worry," he said, nodding to her breasts as if reading her mind. "I won't be touching them for a while."

Her body bounced on the mattress. He slowly crawled over her, shirtless, pants unzipped to release the pressure. A pink tongue traced around her belly button before heading farther down. "Are you okay? Tell me how you feel."

"I-I-I," her voice stuttered, trembling. "I want more." Instantly, her body was eager for his touch again, wanting that second coming.

The tip of his tongue lapped up the juices on the side of her thighs before gently tracing around her other lips, as if preparing for a long kiss.

"Ah!" she panted. "Ooo. Mmm." Her body wiggled against the motions of his tongue, excitement steadily building. Then it darted inside, moving in and out a few times before settling on playing with her sensitive nub.

This wave took less time to peak than the previous one had. The lashing of a relentless tongue kept the momentum going until her limbs trembled from the power of her convulsions.

He sat back on his heels, towering over her. "See, you can do it."

Rip!

A condom?

He was masterful in the way it glided over his shaft. That part was undeniable. Sex wasn't exactly on her mind though. Sleep was.

"You don't want to?"

A different sort of wave rushed over her—guilt. He'd done nothing but pleasure her all evening, despite this encounter being about his fantasies.

"Can I?" she asked. "Won't I be dry after all that?"

He shook his head. "You've only had two orgasms this evening."

"How many do you expect me to have?" she asked.

"Women can have upward of twenty in a single encounter," he said.

"Twenty?!" she exclaimed. "I thought we were starting slow."

"We are," he chuckled, slowly crawling back across her. "I thought we'd aim for four." His mouth swallowed her words before they formed. By the time they came up for air, she'd forgotten what they were. "Are you going to make me beg?"

Instinctively, her legs circled around his waist, drawing him near and leaving his penis poised to enter her. The heat was already building again, albeit touching overstimulated erogenous zones wasn't fuelling the fire. This was a different type of stimulation born from the desire to please.

The tip sat at her entrance, not moving. The sheer restless feeling created a new form of longing, pushing all the right buttons. Her ass wiggled underneath him, but he kept the same distance between them.

"What?" he asked, smirking.

"Stop teasing me," she whispered back.

"But teasing is what makes this part fun," he replied, lining her neck with a necklace of delicate kisses. "The more I wait, the more you want it."

"I already want it," she said, chest heaving up and down from breathlessness.

A slight push, and even more of him was inside her. Her lower half squirmed, trying to do the work for him. The reward was another slight push.

"Isn't it driving you crazy?" she asked.

"I told you," he replied. "I like to watch. I enjoy seeing you want more."

"I can't take it!" she exclaimed, teeth grating over her bottom lip. "Please. Take me. I want to feel all of you inside me."

As if on cue, he put force behind a pelvic thrust, balls

smacking against her ass. He pulled out all the way again, before going for a second balls-deep entry. The pace picked up. Heat building from the friction.

"Oh!" she moaned, watching the expression on his face change as he neared climax. "Yes! Harder! Harder!" Her body stiffened in uncontrollable spasms, the feeling of his climax driving her over the edge.

They'd done it! They'd actually had sex!

"Drink this." A glass of water returned with him from the bathroom. "You need the fluids."

She took a sip, wetting her lips.

"More," he insisted, rolling on another condom.

"What are you doing?" she asked, turning to place the glass on a nightstand.

The opportunity wasn't lost. He embraced her from behind, whispering gently in one ear ,"I said four. By my count you are only at three."

She gasped. "You can't be serious. My lady parts are all too stimulated to take anymore." She chuckled nervously.

"Not all." The bedroom voice was back. "I can think of a place I haven't touched yet." Fingers traced her ass, sliding between the crack of her butt to a never yet explored jewel. Her body reacted with an immediate twitch of excitement. "Can I?"

Curiosity took the better of her. Would it hurt? Would it feel good? Were the sensations different from everything she'd felt so far?

"If you want me to stop..."

"No," she blurted out. "I want to try. I'm a bit nervous though."

"I can tell," he said, the tip of a finger pushing its way inside, pressure building "You need to fully relax. If you tense up, it will hurt."

She nodded.

"I'm going to use some lubricant." His hand moved away, coming back a moment later. This time the pressure was less, a single finger gliding in and out easily. "Do you like that?"

"Mmm," she groaned, albeit not fully convinced. It felt good, but any thicker and there was bound to be pain involved.

"We'll take it slow," he said, adding a second finger to the one already probing inside her. "Don't clench."

It was hard not to. This new sensation was intense. There was discomfort. There was pleasure. There was an anticipation growing as to what his dick would feel like.

"I won't go any further until you are ready," he said.

"I am," she blurted out. She wanted to explore all the possibilities. This was one of them. "I want to try."

More lube went inside, preparing for the main event. This time it wasn't about teasing. This time he went slow to cause as little pain as possible.

Burning.

He slid in and out, building speed, her butt sucking his cock with every thrust. Her fingers grabbed handfuls of sheets, holding on as he took her completely. The feeling of his release brought a new sensation. Every spasm erupting inside her was felt, sending her over the edge. Intense waves of deep pleasure made their way throughout even the deepest recesses of her core. Full body orgasms were different creatures from the other types she'd experienced.

He pulled out, heading straight to the bathroom.

"Ow!" Even rolling over hurt.

"Are you okay?" he asked, returning. "Did I get a little too rough with your body?"

"No," she said, huffing. "I liked it. Will it hurt this much every time?"

He sat on the bed beside her, pulling open a drawer. "Try using this for a while?"

"What is it?" she asked.

"A butt plug," he answered. "It'll help stretch things a bit."

"I guess I have some homework," she mused. A moment later, all the strength from her body was gone. Sleep came for her.

CHAPTER THIRTEEN
LEEONA

Sex. It filled her mind. It took over her thoughts. What was next? What would make it better? She was a kid who'd never tasted sugar, set free in a candy shop with unlimited funds. Of course, she wanted to try it all. Of course, there'd be some flavours which weren't to her taste. There were bound to be plenty that were though.

He was the candy man offering her samples, or at least would be once the photo shoot was over. For the moment she'd have to settle for a sexy Santa.

There it was again, the feeling of anticipation. Waiting for her doctor to emerge from the dressing room was slowly eating away at her from the inside out. Usually, she wasn't an impatient person, but getting antsy over even the slightest chance of seeing him was quickly becoming the new norm.

What was he going to be wearing?

How much skin was going to be showing?

How sexy were the other people in the room going to find him?

How sexy was she going to find him?

The last one was a no-brainer. The man could wear an oversized tracksuit and still be considered the hottest guy alive by her.

He wouldn't though.

In the short time they'd been acquainted, she'd learned enough about him to know he always dressed to impress, even in the bedroom.

"Ah." Lenny sighed, walking in late. "I'm glad you found someone. I was worried for you for a minute there. My assistant says he's the best of the lot too. Is that true?"

"He is," she agreed.

"That's impressive," Lenny said, tinkering with the position of a few items on the set. Everything was fluffy and white. "There were quite a few lookers in the bunch." He leaned closer to her, lowering his voice. "I've ordered a few copies of the calendar for myself." He adjusted a few lights.

"We appreciate the support," she replied with a grin. "You have all the pictures, I'm sure you didn't have to pay us for copies."

"No. No." One hand waggled at the wrist. "That would go against the terms of the contracts. Photos taken by me for this project can only be used for the charity calendar. Besides, it's for the kids." He gasped; jaw dropped, mouth hanging wide open. "Mmm. That is a nice note to end the year on. Where have you been hiding?"

"At the hospital," she answered. "He's a doctor. We are making a calendar of just doctors from Eastport General."

Stephen was wearing a classic Santa hat and not much more, going shirtless with tight silky red boxers trimmed in white. The fit was snug like a glove made especially with his nether region in mind, leaving little to the imagination of onlookers, especially since he was partially hard. Apparently, watching wasn't all he enjoyed. Being watched seemed just as stimulating.

"Well." Chin rested between the photographer's thumb and forefinger. "Don't get too excited, stud." A pink tongue popped out, wetting his lips. "We can't have anything popping out unexpectedly in the shoot, now can we?" He chuckled under his breath. "Of course, if you'd like a private, more naughty shoot, that can be arranged. I'm happy to rearrange my schedule."

She shot him a scrutinizing glare. He was going to cancel the charity calendar, but would be happy to work overtime for some risqué pictures of Dr. December?

"Perhaps another time," Stephen said. "Unfortunately, my appointment book is filled for quite some time."

"I look forward to it," Lenny replied. "Shall we begin? I'd like you to lie on the white pelt. Oh! Don't worry, it just looks real. It's all fake. Real fur is taboo these days. On your tummy, please." Once his instructions were complied with, he circled his model, taking in every angle, every position.

Lenny put on a show, demonstrating exactly what a professional photographer was supposed to be—a cameraman well versed in the way of the lens—who was in control of every detail. He knew exactly the way he wanted a picture taken, why he wanted a model photographed in a certain way, and which equipment was best.

"Like this?" Stephen asked, his butt jutting up and down during the search to find a comfortable position.

"Mm-hmm. Lift your head." A pillow covered in the same white faux-fur as all the other props slid under the doctor's chin. "Hug it a little." He motioned with one finger for his assistant to start the session.

Despite this being her project, it was her first time in a photography studio watching the magic come to life.

The constant clicking threw her off.

"It's the mechanical shutter," Lenny said, noting the expression of confusion. "It closes at the end of the exposure." One hand went up. Everything immediately halted. He strolled over, checking the pictures on the digital camera. Film was rarely developed anymore. "Hmm. Not bad. Not bad. It might be a little too much though." A brisk walk back to the model saw the fur removed completely, the pillow plain, left without a case. "Can you look straight forward?"

Stephen nodded.

"Go again." Lenny returned to the camera for another look. "Can we add a few small wrapped gifts in front, and let's get some of those glorious muscles in the shot as well."

Leeona sighed. They certainly were glorious.

Lenny examined the latest batch of pictures. "I think we got it," he said with a quirky smile. "That's the fastest of the lot. Thanks for coming in, everyone." He pointed to Stephen. "You, my good man, can go change."

"That's it. Really?" Leeona asked.

"Yes," Lenny replied, glancing at his watch. "I can still make my afternoon tea." Keys dangled in front of her face. "Lock up for me, would you? You can give these to Minerva when you see her next. I have another set at home."

"You trust me with all this?" She swivelled around, seeing why. Lenny's team was already packing up all the equipment.

"It'll just be the bare bones," Lenny explained directly into one ear from behind. "Just give the handle a good jiggle to make sure it's tightly locked. Thank you." With one hand over his head waving, he simply left.

"Okay." Before the word was finished, she was all alone.

Sneak a peek? The thought was short-lived. The good doctor was already changed and ready to hit the road.

What was she supposed to do with all those pent-up desires?

Hormones were rampaging out of control, along with the growing heat between her legs. Everything was building. The pot needed to be stirred before it boiled over. The studio probably wasn't the right place though. There was, however, a plan in place in her mind; one which hatched before the shoot began.

CHAPTER FOURTEEN
LEEONA

THE UNDERGROUND GARAGE WAS A PLACE THE SUN'S RAYS NEVER reached. Artificial light acted as a substitute, but even it was poor. Most of the parking spots were under a low dimmer at best.

The atmosphere was practically set for them.

They were the last two to leave the studio, so vehicles were few and far between. The vibrantly red Jeep stuck out like a sore thumb, but there was no one around to notice.

Like a gentleman, he opened the passenger side door for her.

"Do the front seats recline?" she asked, not making any attempt to get in. "I mean all the way back? They do, don't they?"

"Yeah," he answered, with a nervous head nod. "There's a lever under the side of the seat and another at the front for leg room. Why?"

"Get in," she ordered, pulling the bar. The seat fell to an almost flat position. "No arguing. Just do it." There was an urgency to her words, one she was sure he'd picked up on. The change in her demeanour wasn't just that single thing. It was a combination of cravings and desires he'd unleashed within her.

Now, he was going to take responsibility for her libido running wild. Once he was in and fully laid back, she straddled him, undoing his belt and the zipper on his pants.

"This isn't going to be as easy as it looks," he said.

"I don't care," she huffed. "I can't wait any longer."

"You are wearing clothes," he said. "I am wearing clothes. Vehicles can be awkward too. Besides, someone might come and see us."

"I like being watched," she whispered in his ear, nibbling gently on the lobe. "You showed me this world and I want to experience all of it. Besides..." She lifted up her skirt. "I'm not wearing any panties."

"You little vixen," he chuckled, hands interlocking behind his neck. "Go on then. Do your worst. I'm ready."

He was. In fact, he was already rock-hard.

Her being on the top was a position they hadn't explored yet. Being in charge was something she'd never considered trying before.

Fingers gripped his shaft, pulling the head out of the opening in his pants. Her hand held it steady, guiding it to a new opening to hide within. Once the tip was in, the rest of her body slid down until all of his penis was fully engulfed.

"Ohh!" she groaned. "Ohh!" The rocking motion began, grinding herself against him, until all the right spots were reached at once. Her movements became faster, breath heavier. "Yes!"

Her hands, now free, made quick work of the buttons on her blouse. It fell to the side without care. The cups on the red bra she'd chosen pulled down, allowing her nipples access to the steamy air around them. He wasn't moving. This was her show and she was determined to put on a good one. Fingers on each hand grabbed a nipple, gently pinching and twisting. As she came close to overflowing, they pulled harder.

"Yes!"

She was almost there, so close to climaxing.

Tap!

Tap!

"Yes!" she screamed. A wave washed over her, orgasm spilling into orgasm.

Tap!

Tap!

Heavy breath left a layer of fog everywhere, but the silhouette of a man standing outside the Jeep was still visible. Stephen reached over to the middle console pressing on a button. The passenger side window went down.

"Ahem," Lenny cleared his throat. "I forgot my wallet inside. I'll need the keys."

Stephen fished them out of her pocket, one hand dangling them outside the window. "These them?" he asked.

"They are," Lenny chuckled. "Sorry to disturb."

"We were just finishing up," he replied, firing off a wink.

She made no effort to move—no attempt to cover up. He was still inside her. Spasms were still contracting around his shaft.

This was cloud nine.

"Don't worry," Lenny said. "I won't tell Minerva about your little parking lot rendezvous. It'll be our little secret."

Bye-bye, cloud nine. She was right back on earth again, both feet planted firmly on the ground. What would the other moms think if they knew about her arrangement with Dr. December? What would they say?

There wasn't an opportunity to answer the photographer or even thank him. He was already gone, leaving her alone with her doctor again.

"I wanted to ask a favour," she said, descending from her cowgirl straddle. "Tommy's doctor wants us to try out a new experimental treatment. I was hoping you'd have a look at the proposal and give me a second opinion."

CHAPTER FIFTEEN
STEPHEN

Air from the underground garage flowed in through the still open door, cooling his body to that of a normal resting state.

She was still dripping sweat, among other bodily fluids, lungs gasping for breath. Their short hook-up session left her weary.

That was the day's lesson.

Being in charge wasn't a breeze. It took work. It took effort. It took stamina. All of hers was fully spent.

Props for not passing out were deserved though. The night before her eyes refused to remain open, leading to a sound sleep. Even come morning, there was no waking her. But then relaxation was pleasure's reward.

"Mixing business with..."

"I know what you are going to say," she blurted out. "It's not politically correct for you, as my current lover, to consult on my son's condition. You're wrong!"

An enigma. That's what she was. One minute she was convulsing around his dick, the next she was talking shop, like nothing had happened.

A full one-eighty in sixty seconds or less.

That wasn't all, either. When she initially stepped into his office, she was inexperienced. Now, she understood her own body. She knew what she wanted and went after it, whether it was sex or something else.

"If a doctor's wife is brought into emergency, does he wait for another doctor to treat her?" she asked. "If the ER is overrun from a multi-car accident, do the doctors not treat the injured because they are previously acquainted? If it were your son, would you walk away?"

"No," he agreed. "But I would step back to let another capable doctor take the lead."

Her lips puffed out, forming a needy pout; eyes darkened by sadness. "I'm not asking you to take over as his doctor. All I want is your opinion."

"Okay," he reluctantly agreed. "I'll give you my personal opinion... nothing on the books. Is that all right?"

"Mm-hmm." Leaning over, her face neared his, their lips lightly brushing against each other.

A reward?

Amazing.

In just a few short meetings, she'd completely mutated. Their first rendezvous saw hers almost toppling over while trying to undress in front of him. Now, she spoke her mind freely, not to mention wasn't wearing underwear and was ready to pounce on a whim. Her confidence levels were at an all-time high. Who knew how high they'd end up soaring?

She certainly wasn't shy anymore, straddling him, breasts exposed, while another person looked on. Even if Lenny was more interested in him than her, there was a certain level of self-assurance needed to pull off being watched in that manner.

The transformation from duckling to swan was exhilarating to watch, and the show was just going to get better as time went on.

Just how curious was she?

Was she willing to fulfill his deepest fantasies?

In medical school, it became obvious that everyone had a fetish of some sort, admitted or not. His was watching. His best friend, Kyle, enjoyed sharing. The two went hand-in-hand, creating some rather spectacular evenings.

Those sensations were all but lost to memories. A part of him believed he'd never feel that way again. It had been years, after all. Then again, it had been years since either of them had a girlfriend.

"Hey, daydreamer," she said. "You gonna lie there all day?" One hand hugged her own hip, the other holding the passenger side door.

"No." The zipper on his pants closed. "I'm moving."

New memories were overwriting others. New pleasures were taking the place of old ones. That wasn't to say he'd given up on asking for a threesome.

It was up to her in the end. She held his strongest wants in the palm of her hand. A simple yes would open up a whole new world for both of them.

Now wasn't the time though. After the decisions about Tommy's treatments had been made, he'd plead his case. Until then, it was business as usual.

CHAPTER SIXTEEN
DR. KENT CAMMBELL'S OFFICE

There was a little yellow duck, wearing a Santa hat and scarf, sitting on his desk. A coincidence? Probably not. There was a good chance it was one of the rubber duckies he'd donated to the pediatric ward. Its new home was in the office of Dr. Kent Cammbell, the top children's oncologist in not only the hospital, but the surrounding areas as well.

If there was a new procedure, or radical type of treatment, he was on top of it. That's what they were there to discuss—a new regimen for Tommy.

"I'm not a quack," Kent said with a smile, quickly realizing no one in the room got his joke. "Ahem. I understand you were the one who donated these little guys. Thanks for that. They've brought a lot of smiles to the faces around here. It's a new level of paying it forward in the duck, duck, Jeep tradition. Duck, duck, hospital? That doesn't sound as good, but I hope it takes off and becomes the new big thing. Spreading a little cheer is always good. A genuine smile is a cure we haven't been able to bottle, but it is an effective pain and stress reliever and it comes without a hefty price tag attached."

"You donated them?" Leeona shrieked. "Ahem." She reeled in

the shock. "Are Tommy's latest results in? Has there been any change?"

Doctor exchanged glances with doctor.

"It's okay," Leeona blurted out. "I asked Dr. Clause to come. He's a friend of mine and I want to cover all my bases." She paused. "It's not that I don't trust you, of course. I do."

Kent chuckled. "That's all right. I fully understand. Tommy is your baby, after all. If it makes you feel better to have Stephen here, that's fine by me." He handed over the boy's medical charts. "It's your consent which is needed. If you want him here, he can stay."

"What's his current condition?" Stephen asked.

"Tommy is stable at the moment," Kent replied. "The cancer hasn't progressed, nor has it shown signs of shrinking. It is my opinion; he may benefit from the latest clinical trial."

"Is it necessary?" she asked.

"No," Kent replied, leaning back in his chair, hands folding together. "But given the current success rate for the new treatment, the fact Tommy's condition is a match to all requirements, and there is no cost to you, I strongly recommend taking part."

"Are there side effects?" Leeona asked

"There is always the possibility of side effects," the doctor replied. "Even with the current treatment plan, there are. You know that. I can't say what they might be. I can only tell you what is in the early reports. Here." He used the edge of the desk to pull forward his rolling chair, placing a sheet of paper in front of her. "That's a list of possible adverse reactions. It is pretty standard stuff."

"I don't know," she said, squeezing her lover's hand with all her might, looking for his support and input.

"Hmm," he groaned, pulling away from her grip. Fingers flexed, relieving the stiffness caused by the earlier extreme pressure. "I can't give professional advice, but I can say the treatment program looks good on paper. I would certainly suggest it to any of my patients, if they were given such an opportunity."

"Really?" Her gaze fell to the floor, intently staring but seeing nothing.

"Look." Kent inhaled deeply. "I can't force you to accept this offer, but I can say it won't come around again. This is a once-in-a-life-time deal, a true one and done. If you don't take the spot, there are hundreds of others who will jump at the opportunity. Think about it, but don't take too long. I can't hold off giving an answer for more than forty-eight hours."

Leeona gasped. "But Christmas is only a few days away. I need to discuss this with Tommy, and I don't want to ruin the season for him."

"He's tougher than you give him credit for," Kent suggested.

"I've only met him once, but I'll agree with that diagnosis," Stephen said. "He's a fighter, who worries just as much about his mother as she does about him. I think you should have a talk with him. Bring Kent with you to explain the fine details. He may be young, but it is his body and he should at least have a chance to express his feelings."

"Okay!" she agreed. "I'll talk to Tommy and have an answer for you tomorrow."

The truth was, as frightening as it was, she'd already decided to accept the offer. It was the season for miracles, after all. This was a present waiting to be opened. Maybe Santa crossed off both Tommy and her own wishes at the same time.

Until the ribbon was pulled, there was no telling what the box actually held. No one refused a gift left under the tree because they were too scared it might not be exactly what they asked for.

CHAPTER SEVENTEEN
STEPHEN

Time flew by. Things were busier than before. In his profession, work came before anything, and anyone else. Lives were held in the palms of his hands, after all. Dropping the ball had real life or death consequences. Fantasies, on the other hand, were still going to be there when all was said and done. Putting pleasure on hold was a necessity. It wasn't going to boil away on the back burner, if he turned it off.

The recliner creaked, tilting to a fully laid-back position for a five-minute, well-deserved rest—just enough time for forty winks.

The images on the backs of shut lids were of her. That had been the total extent of their contact over the past few weeks. A situation which couldn't be helped.

She was just as busy as he was, especially with calendar sales. Apparently, they were going like hotcakes.

Fingers rubbed weary eyes, bringing slightly blurred vision back into alignment. His gratuitous copy was lying in a pile to the right side of his desk; the plastic still intact. There was no desire to look at any of it. He certainly wasn't interested in seeing colleagues half-naked, and his own photo was his worst nightmare come true.

The whispering in the corridors.

The eyes, picturing him wearing little to nothing but that Santa hat.

The soft giggles.

The playful flirtatious banter.

He never wanted any of it when he wasn't seeing anyone. Now that he was, his interest levels plummeted even farther.

"It's for a good cause," her voice said in his mind.

There was no arguing that point. After taking his first tour of the children's ward, it was evident they were lacking a lot of things. Children needed mental stimulation to grow. It was as important as diet, exercise, and proper medical care.

The hospital dropped the ball in that regard. Too bad it wasn't the bouncy type kids were able to play with.

He considered going to the brass, but if Kent wasn't able to get more funding for the department he worked in, a doctor from another sector wasn't going to be able to convince them.

Red tape. The stuff was everywhere, sticking to walls, floors, needles, pills, people. There was no escaping it. Cut a piece and a hundred more would appear to patch the spot up.

Eastport General was lucky to have the moms. They were picking up the slack that the hospital left for trash.

He picked up a file.

"Oh." It was Tommy's. Kent must have sent it for him to review. "Hmm." The patient was responding well to the treatment. The cancer showed signs of shrinkage. If the trend continued, there'd be a good chance Leeona would be taking him home come spring.

It was too early to share that sort of news though. Statistics were merely numbers. There were always extreme cases on either side of the spectrum. The only certainty was this disease was unpredictable. There were patients diagnosed with a few months left, who went on to live another ten or twenty years. There were also those who should have thrived but died instead.

Getting the hopes up of loved ones was cruel.

He tucked the folder beneath his own stack of files. Each of his patients had families waiting for them to come home. Each of his patients were desperate for good news. There was too little to go around, especially for the most magical time of the year.

If only he was the real deal, pulling cures out of the red sack slung over a shoulder. He wasn't though. His name was spelled with an e at the end.

"All it takes is to believe," he said out loud. There was some basis of fact in that statement. It was the same as mind over matter.

It wasn't a cure-all.

It wouldn't work for everyone.

But... if a person truly believed in themselves, there was always the chance.

Maybe Saint Nick was just a way to let those hopes manifest. Maybe the idea behind the jolly old man wasn't a bad one. Maybe sharing the same name wasn't such a burden, after all.

CHAPTER EIGHTEEN
STEPHEN

Christmas Eve.

It was a crisis no one was prepared for. The Santa hired for the children's ward party cancelled at the last minute and kept the already-paid fee. With only a few hours' notice, finding another suitable Saint Nick was impossible. There were no options to explore.

"Who was in charge of hiring Santa?" Leeona bellowed. She wasn't the same meek gal who crocheted items while being belittled just a few weeks ago. Now, her voice was heard. Her opinions mattered. She was a strong, independent woman and everyone knew it.

"I was," Menerva admitted. "He came recommended by a trusted source. I have no idea what happened."

"We got scammed," Gerty, a new mom in the group, hissed. "That's what happened. You should have checked him out before paying him."

"Or paid him after the job was done!" Leeona exclaimed.

"He needed the money to buy Christmas gifts for his kids,"

Menerva argued. "He was in the same bind as we are. Of course, I believed him. Who goes around thinking everyone is out to get them?"

"Normal people," Gerty huffed.

He slipped away while the women were squabbling, heading to the dreaded basement and the room of useless items, or mostly useless since one piece of the hoarded garbage was actually needed.

The bear stared him down, unwilling to give up its treasure quite so easily. It leaned to the left. He went the opposite way, grabbing a still sealed package right out from under its nose.

Timber!

The race was on. The bear toppled over, hitting a rather large pile of sequined lab coats. What they were for was anyone's guess. After that, the domino effect came into play.

He ducked right, narrowly missing being hit by flying rubber bats. The course changed, veering left at the mountain of what he hoped were fake spiders, but who knew? They might have been the real deal, nesting among the mess.

It was hard to ascertain the truth about anything once the dust was disturbed. Tiny particles floated down in no hurry to return to the spots from whence they came. Individually, they were almost invisible to the naked eye. In large quantities, however, they obscured not just vision, but all of the senses.

"Achoo."

His nose wasn't running fast enough. It had been caught. The rest of him still had a chance. The exit was in reach—only a few more steps.

Both arms rose over his head. "Goal!" He made it, barely, but he escaped the wrath of the giant teddy bear unscathed for the most part and with the treasure.

Ding!

The elevator doors were slow to open.

"Where have you been?" Leeona gasped, covering her mouth with one hand. "Where did you find that get up?"

"Gag gifts," he replied, fixing the white beard and moustache. "Is it straight? How does it look? I didn't have a mirror."

"It looks fine," Leeona replied. "I thought you hated the whole Santa thing."

"I do," Stephen admitted "Or, I did. I figure I might as well go with the flow. I have a feeling that calendar picture is going to be around for a lot longer than a year."

"Oh, yeah," two voices said at the same time, Lenny and Jordan exchanging glances.

"Did you two come to pick up your orders?" Leeona asked. "I am curious. You both ordered more than one copy."

"One for the basement, while watching movies," Lenny said.

"One for the bathroom, one for the bedroom," Jordan added.

"One to ruin on the very first night," Lenny chuckled.

"So, they aren't gifts?" Leeona's brow arched.

"Oh, they are," Jordan said, fingers snapping. "These are gifts for myself. The money goes to a good cause. I'm happy. The kids are happy." One finger extended toward the man with whom the passion was shared. "Are you happy? I think you are, but I'll ask anyway."

"I'm pretty happy," Lenny agreed.

"Lenny is the photographer," Leeona explained.

"Really!" Jordan exclaimed. "I would've just kept a few pictures for myself."

"I can't do that," Lenny said. "There are contracts in place to stop me from exploiting the models. The job is a thrill though."

"I would love to hear all about it," Jordan said, intertwining their arms. "Maybe I could book a shoot some time."

The two strolled off down the hall to the designated party room. She heard them entering from down the hall.

"Yoo-hoo," Jordan whistled, joining the party as if it were thrown for him in classic Jordan style. "I just wanted to drop in and say hello." He strutted in, motioning for Lenny to follow. "I'm normally stuck down in emergency, but have a small break, so I thought I'd come see you all." Everyone knew him, the orderly with flair, always searching for love, but never finding the right man.

"I hope that works out for them," Leeona said, cracking a grin. "And thank you for being our Santa. You look oddly sexy with a big belly and a white beard."

"Thanks, I think," he said. "A guy who eats billions of cookies in a single night probably shouldn't be a role model for kids everywhere."

"Don't spoil the mood."

He jumped. The smack on his ass wasn't anticipated. "Hey, now. I have to sit on that tush for an entire night in a cold sleigh. Don't make things any worse."

"Go spread some joy," she chuckled. "The kids are waiting."

He slung a big red sack over one shoulder. "Afterward, how about we spread some joy together?" He added a suggestive wink.

"Do a good job and I'll throw in something much better than milk and cookies," she replied. "I might even let you unwrap your present early."

Laughter filled the halls for the next hour. The kids were happy. The visitors were happy. Leeona was happy.

And for once, on Christmas, he was happy.

CHAPTER NINETEEN
LEEONA

The holidays were over. Everything on her list was checked off. There was nothing left to ask for. Tommy's health was improving. There was a man in her life. And, she'd found herself, after digging out from under layers and layers of lies and misconceptions. Nothing was weighing her down anymore. Nothing was holding her down either. She'd been freed, mentally, physically, and sexually. It wasn't the end of the journey though. There was more to learn. There was more to experience. Stephen was the gateway to all of it. His suggestions were always spot-on... but this latest proposal came out of left field, blindsiding her. She'd never considered the possibility.

She enjoyed being watched. Just the idea of experiencing new sensations was thrilling. The question was: how much more was she ready for?

"We've talked about this," he said. "If you have any doubts, the evening's plans stop right here, right now. There is no pressure... no one is forcing you."

"I know," she replied. "I've had plenty of time to think it over, and I want to." Trying new things was what life was all about. It took her twenty-eight years to figure that out. Marrying as a teen because of a pregnancy was the biggest mistake of her life, not that she'd change a thing given the chance. Tommy was born from that union. He was her pride and joy. Being his mother was her true calling.

Knock. Knock.

It was time. She inhaled deeply, moving to the spot she first stood in front of Stephen, with the same rush washing over her. It was the not knowing—it was the curiosity—it was the anticipation, and every second of it left her dripping from exhilaration.

"Come on in," Stephen said, shaking a man's hand.

First impressions were key to all of them. She needed to spark interest in him and vice versa for the night's activities to go off without a hitch.

"Have a seat. I'll grab drinks. Your usual okay?" Stephen asked.

"Mmm," his friend responded, not taking his eyes off of her.

"Leeona, this is my good friend, Kyle," Stephen said, his back to them at the mini-bar. He turned around briefly, eyes twinkling with the same excitement she was feeling.

She nodded a silent greeting. Introductions were a formality. Regardless of knowing his name, he was a stranger—a stranger who was about to have her in any way he wanted—a stranger who was about to be the third man to be inside her.

Stephen poured drinks—whisky on the rocks. He sat on one side of the sofa, while his friend took the other side, discussing old times as if she wasn't even there. His head turned mid-sentence, intensely gazing at her. "Leeona, why don't you strip?"

Her entire body flushed with a heightened sensitivity, heat increasing between her legs, nipples tingling as they stiffened.

This was it.

The best night of her life was about to begin.

All the preparations for this part were left up to her. Complicated wasn't sexy. She'd made it simple. The silk robe which had been her sole protection against lust-filled eyes fell, forming a pile around her feet.

"So this is the girlfriend," Kyle said, standing. "Not much on theatrics, huh?" Every step he made was carefully executed—the theatrics he'd mentioned. In this evening's production, his role was clear. He was a pack alpha, forming a bond. Once in place, there'd be no defying him. She'd be willingly at his mercy.

A quick glance at Stephen told her no help was coming from him.

"How many?" Kyle asked.

"Four," Stephen replied.

"Just four?" Kyle mused. "We can do better than that." One hand grabbed a breast, gently massaging it. "I'm thinking at least seven or eight."

She gasped, the realization of what the two men were discussing finally registering. Four was the most times she'd climaxed in a single night. That was on the verge of insane. Now, these two were planning on doubling it.

"Move in front of Stephen," Kyle whispered in her ear, one hand still playing with her breast, the other pushing her gently on the back to position her exactly the way he wanted—within touching distance of both men. "It doesn't take much to get this little rabbit ready, does it?" His fingers fell between her legs. A second later, two were inside her, probing her most private area. "Join me." His instructions weren't limited to just her; he was telling Stephen what to do as well.

No time was wasted in following his friend's lead. Her stance widened at his touch, allowing both men to finger her at the same time.

"Oh!" she panted. "Wow!" The feeling of having two different sets of fingers, alternating pushing in and out at the same time, sent her spiralling over the edge.

"One." Kyle said, chuckling. A light touch from him was

enough to move her body. "Head on Stephen's lap," he instructed.

She complied, as if his words were the only option, her mind still reeling, juices still flowing. Her legs fell open, exposing herself to him. Instantly, his tongue took over for the fingers. The licking, flicking, and sucking began.

"How does she taste?" Stephen asked, using his time for a little nipple play. He pinched, she moaned. He twisted, she groaned.

"Delicious," Kyle replied.

That one word sent waves rippling through her body, his mouth keeping the contractions going. A condom passed over her head.

Rip.

She knew the sounds. He was getting ready to take her while her body was still flowing with erotic spasms.

"Two," Kyle snickered, pushing inside her in one thrust. "How does it feel to have a stranger inside you?" He pumped harder. "How does it feel to know your lover is watching another man go balls deep in your pussy?"

"Ooo!" she screamed.

He stopped moving for a moment. "Do you like my dick?" he asked.

She squirmed not wanting to answer, but the need for him to move growing intensely.

"Tell me you want me!" he insisted. "Tell me how good my dick feels. Tell me in front of your lover how much you want me to continue."

Stephen said nothing.

She was too far in the throes of passion to defy him. "It feels good. Please! I want more. I want it faster. I want it harder. Take all of me."

He chuckled, thrusting deep inside her. "That's a good girl," he said. "Keep begging the stranger to screw you."

Inhibition flew out the window. "I want to feel you come!" she screamed, feeling her own climax begin.

He pulled out. "Not yet," he said. "That was only three. There's plenty of time to feel me lose my load inside you. Don't worry. I may plan on taking my time enjoying my best-friend's woman, but I assure you, you will feel me come! I am going to leave my mark on you; one your lover won't be able to erase. By the end of the night, you'll be screaming my name, not his." He glanced over at Stephen. "Let's move to the bedroom. I have a few more things to try. Did you bring the toys?"

Toys? What toys were they talking about, as if she wasn't even there?

Stephen nodded. "I made a treasure chest. Use whatever you like on her."

"Are you holding out okay?" Kyle asked.

"Mmm," Stephen nodded, carrying her like a princess to the other room. "I may need to jump in soon, but I want to hold off for as long as I can."

"You always did prefer one big explosion to several little firecrackers," Kyle said.

Her body gently floated down the bed, rather than being tossed on there like a rag doll—the calm before the storm. Her stranger wasn't a stranger anymore. In the past hour, she'd come to know him intimately. That's why watching him rummage through a small wooden box of toys was both frightening and thrilling all rolled up in one, much the same feeling as going on a roller coaster for the first time.

She turned over, not wanting to see what was coming. That was a mistake. Her own lack of vision chose the pleasure aid for them.

The squeezing of the tube.

The feeling of the lube.

The little pink gem on her bottom puckered, clenching then

releasing as fingers probed around the outside. Then the cold of silicone stretched her hole open.

"What is that?" she asked, gasping.

"A little bullet," Kyle whispered. Vibrations began low and steady. "Don't worry, it's made from body safe material, and..." He snickered. "...doctor recommended. It's meant to expand the area while stimulating at the same time and won't go all the way in. I thought it was time we got your body ready for double penetration."

"Double penetration?" she echoed.

One hand reached around, playing with her sensitive nub. "It's time to tie the record," he whispered in her ear from behind. The vibrations increased threefold, letting her know he was in charge.

CHAPTER TWENTY
LEEONA

Number four left her tingling. Much the same as her first time experiencing multiple climaxes, most of her body was overstimulated.

"Drink," Stephen said, handing her a glass of ice water. He was still fully clothed, albeit with a bulge in his pants.

Lips smacked, tongue exploring the cavern of her mouth. It was completely dried out and screaming for even a trickle of liquid, yet she hadn't noticed until he told her. The first sip was pure luxury, moisture coating lips, teeth, and tongue, but just a tease. She inhaled deeply before taking the rest in one swig. A cool sensation travelled to the back of her throat, the water sliding its way down in gulps.

"Easy," Stephen chuckled. "There is plenty more."

Her arm became a napkin, wiping the bits of liquid which hadn't made the voyage with the rest from her face. "More." The glass extended, only a few cubes remaining at the bottom.

"I think it's time to clean up a bit," Kyle said. "Do you mind if I take her in the bathroom for a bit?"

"Be my guest," Stephen said.

"Come on then." Kyle winked playfully. "It'll give your body a chance to relax." He placed her glass on the nightstand. "You can drink the shower water, if you want."

"You want me to move?" she asked, brow arching. She was lucky to still be awake.

"Yeah," Kyle laughed, gripping one arm tightly. All it took was a slight pull to bring her to her feet, legs surprisingly stable.

"But..." She glanced over at Stephen for instruction. There was none coming. He was laid back on the bed, hands locked behind his head without any signs of moving.

"No buts," Kyle said. "It's just you and me."

He was supposed to watch. He was supposed to be a party to their activities. So far Stephen hadn't contributed much to the evening's romp. Now, she was alone with Kyle in a different room.

"We won't be long," he said, letting the tap run. Water cascaded over his fingers. "Hop in. It's quite warm."

One foot followed the other; a waterfall and multiple jets hitting her skin at the same time. The stream fell over her head, face and shoulders, washing away fatigue. Even her erogenous zones were feeling rejuvenated.

"Peppermint or cinnamon?" Kyle asked, holding up two bottles of body wash.

"Peppermint," she answered without thought. That minty-fresh feeling left by using toothpaste and mouthwash was the jewel in her crown when it came to hygiene rituals.

He stepped in behind her. "Peppermint it is." He began slowly, lathering up her skin, before moving on to any parts which might be still sensitive.

"Mmm," she moaned, enjoying the feeling of all her cares being washed away. "Whoa!" Eyes opened wide to a creeping sensation, offering a pleasing tingle all over her body. "What is this?"

"Peppermint," he mused. "You chose it."

"If I had picked cinnamon?" she asked.

"A warming sensation," he replied, stepping out for a moment.

Zip.

A black bag opened.

"What now?" she asked.

"A little landscaping," he said, returning with a razor and scissors, and taking one knee in front of her. "It's not a proven science, but from my experience, women have increased sensations directly related to the amount of pubic hair they have. Don't worry, I won't leave you bald eagle. I'm just going to tidy things up a bit. Spread 'em."

He spoke and her legs moved as if they were his own.

"Stay still," he instructed, the razor gliding close to her inner thigh. "Just a bit more off the top. It's just like having a trim, isn't it?"

Teeth grated over her bottom lip. Having a trim never felt that good before.

"Okay," he said, still facing her nether region, "it's time for the test."

"Test?" she asked. "Oh." His tongue was already probing all the freshly shaved areas. He was right. It was more sensitive now.

He stood, lifting her off the floor, her back pressed against a tile wall. Instinctively, legs wrapped around him, his thick shaft penetrating her like a spear. It was sharp. It was hard. It was intense. It was divine.

"He's not here," he whispered in her ear, thrusting in and out. "He isn't watching. This is just the two of us. Do you like screwing another man?"

She gasped. That wasn't the plan. This was about the three of them enjoying a sexual experience together. Why hadn't Stephen joined them? Why had she forgotten he was still on the bed?

"You don't have to answer." He bit the lobe of her ear. "I

already know you like it. You want me to fill you with my cum. Don't worry, I slipped a condom on while I was grooming you." He plunged in harder, farther. "Scream my name!"

She was a puppet, and he held all the strings. It wasn't the same as with Stephen. He was in charge but always asked for her input, and considered her feelings. Kyle was all about control. When he spoke, she reacted. Her body was his to do with as he pleased.

"Kyle!" The next climax came at the same time.

"Again!" he demanded. "Make it loud enough for Stephen to hear. I want him to know the fifth time was all me."

"Kyle!"

His body shuddered. She felt every bit of his intense orgasm.

"Good girl," he praised. "Let's go see what your lover is up to. I hope he's not mad." A sly grin crossed his lips. "Don't worry. You still have at least one more in you. Once you come for him, everything will be right as rain."

CHAPTER TWENTY-ONE
LEEONA

Surely, he wasn't mad. How could he be? This whole evening was his idea. He let her go into the shower with another man naked. He knew what was going to happen.

She peeked out from the bathroom door, before being pushed from behind right into the spotlight. Or it would have been the centre of attention, if Stephen hadn't stolen it. All of his rich skin was showing as he lay naked, one hand rubbing his hard penis.

"I thought you two were going to take forever," he said. "I was getting a bit bored, waiting."

"Sorry," Kyle replied. "I just needed to remind her who was in control this evening. I don't think she quite understood that it's not her, and it's not you. I'm pretty sure the message came through loud and clear though." He plopped down on the bed beside his friend.

"That might be true," Stephen sighed, "but I am tired of waiting. I'm at my limit." He glanced directly in her direction. "Get on top."

She rushed over, straddling him as he directed his penis to her hole. It slid in easily. "That's it," he said. "Up and down. Not too fast." He pulled her hair, forcing her body toward his. "Don't stop."

She felt Kyle move behind her, his fingers covered in lube, probing her ass, then the tip of his penis applied pressure.

"Ah!" she screamed as he slowly pushed farther in. Two men were inside her at once. Two men were screwing her relentlessly, and all she could do was moan, groan, and scream.

"Stephen!" His name needed to be first. "Kyle!" He was bound to punish her in some way for forgetting him. "Damn!"

Her body stiffened, preparing for a large release. Euphoric contractions were followed by tingly sensations, similar to that produced by the shower gel, all over the surface of her skin. Legs shook involuntarily. She had no idea if either of her partners climaxed at the same time. All of her was too numb to tell.

"Oh well," Kyle said, climbing off. "It looks like six was all she wrote." He gently rolled her body off his friend, the two men disappearing into the bathroom together.

She was more wearisome than exhausted. None of her muscles would move, but sleep hadn't come for her.

"He's gone," Stephen said, crawling into the bed, and tossing one arm over her. "I saw him out."

"Oh," she said. Just like that, Kyle was a stranger again.

"I thought you'd be in la-la land by now," he replied. "Is everything okay?"

"Yeah," she answered softly. "I was just wondering, is this going to be a regular thing now? I mean, will Kyle be joining us often?"

"Often?" he echoed. "No. Too much of a good thing can become boring. I was thinking of keeping Kyle's visits a treat." He placed a small red box on the bed directly in front of her face. "Happy birthday."

She turned enough to meet his gaze. "You knew? But how?"

"Mmm." He nodded. "Tommy told me. Go on. Open it."

The lid popped open, revealing a set of diamond stud

earrings. "They're beautiful," she said. "Thank you. You didn't have to."

"I wanted to," he replied, rolling to his usual position on his back, hands behind his head. "Next year," he said, nodding. "It was too soon this year, but next year, I'll buy you a ring."

She popped up. "You're serious?"

"Mm-hmm." He reached up, gently stroking her face. "We are a good match. You seem surprised though."

"I thought you might be mad about... you know?"

His brow arched. "About what?"

"The bathroom," she muttered meekly. "I had sex with Kyle in there."

"You had sex with Kyle all night," Stephen mused. "I invited him, remember?"

"Yeah, but you weren't there." She shrugged. "And I know I didn't have to, but I did. I wanted to. Isn't that wrong?"

"Not at all," Stephen replied. "I created a safe environment for you to explore those feelings. I made it possible for you. Now, if you were to go behind my back and screw a bunch of random guys, I'd be upset."

"So this was all for me?" she asked.

"Well," Stephen replied, "I enjoyed myself as well. Watching you go from cold to hot then climax is the best sort of stimulation for me. You could say I get off on watching you find pleasure. Like I said though, I don't want this feeling to become normal. I want it to be special. That's why I'll let you have Kyle on special occasions or celebrations... the honeymoon excluded."

She turned fully over, cuddling into his chest. "I'm glad I found you, Stephen Clause."

"I'm glad you did too."

CHAPTER TWENTY-TWO
ONE YEAR LATER...

Ding. Dong.

She rushed to the door to let their guest in. The life of firsts with Stephen kept on giving. This was her first guest, at her first holiday party, in the first home of their own.

"Pina!" Her arms tossed around her sister's neck.

"Uh." She struggled to carry bags of gifts and the weight of her sister through the threshold. "Mind if I come in first? It's snowing."

Leeona released her grip, taking a look outside before closing the door. "I thought it was going to be a completely green Christmas."

"That just goes to show you, life is full of surprises," Stephen said, rubbing his hands together. "Can I take your coat?"

"Thanks," Pina replied, handing it, with her hat and scarf tucked neatly in a sleeve, over. "Tommy! Come give your aunt a hug."

The clinical trial had been a complete success. He'd been home for over six months without issue. The cancer was in remission, with no signs of returning. He was even enrolled in a regular school for the following fall.

Ding!

Leeona answered the door.

"Uncle Kyle!" Tommy exclaimed, jumping into the man's arms.

"Pfft." Pina glanced the other way. "I don't even get a hi, let alone a hug... and I've always been his favourite aunt."

"You're his only aunt," Leeona said.

Tommy motioned with one finger for her to bend down. His arms wrapped around her neck tightly. "I love you too."

"I hope I'm not late," Kent said, peeking around the crowd from the front porch.

"Not at all." Stephen cleared the way, taking coats and ushering everyone into a bigger room. "Have a seat. You can introduce yourselves. I'll get the holiday cheer." By holiday cheer, he meant drinks. No one drove, and if anyone was going to be the designated driver, it was him.

"Sounds good," Kent said, rubbing his hands together. "I'll have..." The host was already gone without taking any orders. "Whatever." He shrugged

A tray returned in Stephen's hands. "Hot buttered rum, spiced eggnog, mulled wine? Take your pick." He handed a glass to Tommy, after placing the others on a coffee table. "And a cherry Christmas mocktail for you." He was having the same thing. "Cheers." Their glasses clanked together.

"Can I open my gifts?" Tommy asked, bouncing up and down on the spot. "Please?"

"Of course you can," Pina said. "Your favourite aunt says it's okay." She handed him a package. "I hope you like it."

He made quick work of the wrapping, tossing it about as it shredded. "A robot! Cool."

"It's remote control," Pina added.

"Did you remember the batteries?" Leeona asked.

"Yikes!" Pina chuckled nervously. "Well, it will be cool after I drop some of those off. Sorry."

"Here, open this," Kyle said. "I promise, you don't need batteries."

"Hmph!" Pina crossed her arms over her chest, obviously confused as to who Kyle was. The man wasn't actually related to Stephen, after all, and their best kept secret.

"I wanted these!" Tommy held a box set of mystery books in the air. The spare room upstairs had become his own little library, with wall-to-wall shelves filled with novels, comics, and anything else readable. "Thank you, Uncle Kyle."

Kyle patted the boy's head. "No problem, kiddo."

"Ahem," Kent cleared his throat. "I also brought a gift," he announced, holding out a plain red paper bag.

Tommy peeked inside without taking the gift. "What is it?"

"Memory games," Kent replied, pulling out the box himself. "Each is a puzzle which needs to be solved. I have to warn you though, they aren't easy. You start with number one and they get harder all the way up to ten."

Tommy's eyes filled with excitement. "Thanks." This time he took the gift. "Can I try one now? Please, Mom?"

"Tomorrow," she answered. "We still have to eat."

Dinner came and went without drama or conflict, lasting about twice as long as a normal supper, after which she tucked Tommy into bed, reading his favourite bedtime story. He was fast asleep by the second page.

"Thanks for watching him," Leeona said, descending the staircase.

Pina shrugged. "Anything for my favourite nephew."

"He's your only nephew," she snorted.

"You and Stephen deserve a little alone time," Pina said, grinning from ear to ear. "Enjoy yourselves. I'll see you in the morning."

Alone time. If only she knew Kyle was joining them in their alone time. Her sister's head would probably pop right off. That would have been something to see, but her lips were sealed.

Their covert get-togethers worked because only the participants knew about them. If anyone else found out, professional reputations might be judged, especially those of the doctors. Not everyone was accepting of their lifestyle choices.

"The designated driver Jeep is about to leave the station," Stephen announced. "I'll make sure you all get to your destination safely."

"Thanks," Kent said, heading out the door.

Kyle's eyebrows rose and fell, quickly squeezing by her to exit next.

"Ladies first," Stephen insisted, closing the door behind them. He opened the rear door for her this time.

"You can sit between us," Kyle said, patting the middle seat.

"What's going on?" she asked, eyes narrowing to slits.

"I've asked for Dr. Cammbell's opinion," Stephen replied. "He's going to try to help with your condition." The engine purred, wipers clearing a small layer of snow from the windshield.

"Condition?" she echoed, climbing over Kyle.

"What was the number?" Kent asked.

"Six," Kyle answered. "We can't seem to make it to that elusive number seven."

"Oh, no." It clicked what was going on. "Stephen isn't driving you home right away, is he?"

"No," Kent answered, removing his glasses. "I am going to be consulting on finding a breakthrough for you. Since Tommy is seeing his regular physician now, and I am no longer treating him, there is no longer any question of morality about engaging in a little after supper exploration of his mother's body. With your consent, of course."

"Role-play, huh?" she smirked. "Do you really think you can help me, Doctor?" she asked, batting her lashes.

"Well, there is never any guarantees in these things," Kent

replied. "With a new treatment plan, I think we can make some progress though."

"I'd like to try it right away," she said, glancing down at the shiny diamond on her ring finger. Stephen proposed the night before. She thought that was the big reveal for the holidays. Now this. Her man was full of surprises.

A new experience awaited.

A new day was coming.

By dawn she needed to be home.

This was going to be one heck of a Christmas, and New Year's was right around the corner. Who knew what plans were being made to ring in the new year with a bang?

Anticipation had her dripping. Hopefully, those feelings never ended. That was the ideal ending to her story.

BONUS

As this series is coming to an end, there was one character who appears in all three of my books, whose story I felt wasn't complete.

Continue reading for Jordan's happily ever after.

JORDAN'S ENDING

It was more of a goblet than a wine glass, made with a golden-coloured metal and adorned with red jewels, albeit fake ones.

"Where there is no wine, there is no love," Lenny said, clanking their glasses together. He took a few sips, before pouring himself another glass.

"Naturally," Jordan replied. He preferred to take his time, noting the colour, the aroma, the clarity, before the first taste. It deserved to be savoured in much the same way life itself was. Oddly enough, that was the only thing he liked taking his time with, and that philosophy was the only real difference between the two of them.

He glanced out at the sea of lights from full-length windows.

"Are you worried they'll be upset we didn't go?" Lenny asked.

"Nah," Jordan replied. "I've watched so many couples form over the years, there's no way even I could party hop through all their holiday events. Besides, I was happy for each of them... envious... but happy. I expect they feel the same for us. What about you? Are you missing spending time with your family this year?"

"Menerva?" Lenny chuckled. "I think she can get on fine without me. The holidays at our house weren't in full swing unless someone broke something and everyone was swearing at each other. Ah! Fond memories."

"This must be boring for you, then," Jordan said, batting his fake long lashes. "It's just you and little ole me."

Lenny moved behind him, arms wrapping around his waist. "I don't find you boring." Kisses grazed his neck.

"Mmm," he moaned, tilting his neck to allow better access. "To think, at one point I was actually depressed, slouched over a bar, and swigging back pink cocktails because I didn't think I'd ever find a lasting relationship." He turned, their faces almost touching. "Then you came along."

"Fate," Lenny said softly, closing the distance between them.

Lips pressed against lips. Mouths parted at the same time. Tongues intermingled, searching out pleasure spots to exchange.

"I am a lucky man," Jordan said, lips swollen from kisses.

"I'm luckier," Lenny replied.

"Yeah, you are," Jordan chuckled with a touch of sass. One finger lightly tapped the tip of his partner's nose.

"I thought you were depressed," Lenny said.

"Not anymore, baby," Jordan replied. "I'm back and even more fabulous than before. There's a skip in my step and a twinkle in both my eyes. You know why?"

"Why?"

"Because I found my true love," Jordan declared, arms stretched out at his sides. "I'm here, living in this miraculous apartment, overlooking all the lights of Eastport, with my soul mate at my side. I never thought I'd make it here. Honestly, for the longest time, I was happy being a man-whore."

"I don't want to hear about your other conquests," Lenny said.

"But you don't mind benefiting from all the experience, right?" he snickered. "I might not be the best cook. I might not be great at cleaning up all the time. I have nasty habits. But when it comes to the boudoir, well..." He chuckled seductively. "...the bedroom is the one place I know I can please."

"I'm aware," Lenny said, picking him up like a princess. "Now that you've got me hard, what are you going to do about it?"

Jordan licked his lips. "Mm-hmm. Ha." He giggled, legs kicking. "Want to go find out?" His pencilled-on brows waggled suggestively. "I have a special treat waiting for Christmas."

"We agreed on no gifts," Lenny said.

"This is just a little something special," His nose wrinkled up in the most adorable manner. "For one night only."

Lenny placed him down gently. "I actually have something for you too." He dropped to one knee, a small velvet box in his hand. The lid snapped open, revealing a dazzling ring. "Marry me."

Jordan gasped, one hand covering his mouth, then fanning the air around him. "Yes. A thousand times, yes."

"Was that a line from a movie?" Lenny mused.

"Who cares?" Jordan jumped into his arms. "Take me, you big brute. Tonight. Tomorrow night. Every night for the rest of our lives."

THE END

ABOUT THE DOCTORS OF EASTPORT GENERAL SERIES

I hope you enjoyed my book, Doctor Clause, which is part of the shared world Doctors of Eastport General.

Would you like to read all of them? Find them here only on Kindle Unlimited.

Come on in and meet the new ER Physicians, Surgeons, Specialists, Residents, and patients that occupy the rooms and halls of the largest hospital on the coast of Rhode Island. You may even run into some of the doctors from Season 1, 2 and 3.

We hope you are ready to fall in love with all the new sexy stories that take place inside the walls of Eastport General Hospital.

Titles from Season 3
    Amy Stephens – Doctor Grinch
    Tracy Broemmer – Doctor Holliday
    CA King – Doctor Clause
    Mel Walker – Doctor Charmer

ABOUT THE DOCTORS OF EASTPORT GENERAL SERIES

    TL Mayhew – Doctor Jingle Bells
    E.M. Shue – Doctor Do-Over
    S.L. Sterling – Doctor Frost

Titles from Season 2
    Doctor Irresistible – Syd Ryan
    Doctor Mistake – Amy Stephens
    Doctor Divine – Tracy Broemmer
    Doctor, Please – Celeste Granger
    Doctor Frank Enstein – CA King
    Doctor Change of Heart – Amber Ghe
    Doctor Rescue – Mel Walker
    Doctor Delectable – TL Mayhew
    Doctor Love – Adryan Hart
    Doctor Danger – Pandora Snow
    Doctor Stuck-Up – A.N. Waugh
    Doctor Sinful – E.M. Shue
    Doctor Right – S.L. Sterling

Titles from Season 1
    Doctor Heartbreak by D.M. Davis
    Doctor Feelgood by Amy Stephens
    Doctor D's Orderly Affair by CA King
    Doctor Trouble by E.M. Shue
    Doctor Temptation by Syd Ryan
    Dueling Doctors by DC Renee
    Doctor Sexy by TL Mayhew
    Doctor Fix-It by Mel Walker
    Doctor One of a Kind by Anjelica Grace
    Doctor Casanova by Emma Nichole
    Dirty Doctor by Amanda Richardson
    Doctor All Nighter by Adora Crooks
    Doctor Desire by S.L. Sterling

ABOUT DOCTOR D'S ORDERLY AFFAIR

Every hospital had at least one—a Dr. D—or the equivalent thereof. The thread which strung them into the same category was their absolute flawlessness. Gender varied from place to place, but at Eastport General the physician in question was a man:

Dr. Desmond Danielson had all the tools necessary for an evening of pure pleasure...

The suave demeanour.

The pearly white smile.

The full head of hair, nary a strand out of place. Not even a tornado could best his style.

He played sports.

He saved lives.

He won trophies and awards.

He was well-read, well-established, and in any clothes other than a medical coat with a stethoscope draped around his neck instead of a scarf, he would have appeared too young for the job. No one even truly knew his age. No one cared.

Everyone loved him. And, of course, he was hotter than the tropics on a blustery afternoon during the peak of summer.

There was only one problem: all that perfection only lasted for one night.

ABOUT DR FRANK ENSTEIN

Dr. Frank Enstein spent years becoming a sought-after cosmetic surgeon, and not for the same reason as others in his field. For him, it wasn't about tits and it certainly had nothing to do with ass. His motives were deeper, purer; something only someone with a similar tragic past would understand. Putting up with long lines of superficial women demanding exuberant changes to perfectly fine bodies was a means to an end, and finally it was all paying off.

An assignment with a new burn unit at Eastport General Hospital was the job he wanted—a place where he could really make a difference.

When a busty barmaid tries to start up a conversation, she threatens to drag him back into the practice he left behind. No matter how attractive she is, that could never happen.

Taking a step backward isn't part of the plan, but perhaps it should be.

ABOUT THE AUTHOR

C.A. King, USA Today Bestselling Author, is the recipient of several awards, including:

The Hamilton Spectator Readers' Choice Award for 2017, 2018 & 2019 in the Best Local Author category; The Brant News Readers' Choice Award for 2017 Best Local Author; Readers' Favorite award in the short story/novella category; the 2017 SIBA Award for Best New Adult; the 2017 SIBA Award for Best Novella; 2018 Readers' Favorite International Book Awards: Gold Medal in the Fiction—Supernatural genre; 2018 Readers' Favorite International Book Awards: Bronze Medal in the Fiction – New Adult genre; 2019 Readers' Favorite International Book Awards: Gold Medal in the Fiction – Supernatural genre; 2019 Readers' Favorite International Book Awards: Gold Medal in the Young Adult – Fantasy – Urban Genre; City of Brantford Featured Artist February 2020; Burlington Post Readers' Choice Award in the Best Local Author Category 2020; Toronto Star Readers' Choice Award in the Best Local Author Category 2020; Cambridge Times Readers' Choice Award in the Best Local Author Category 2020; Burlington Post Readers' Choice Award in the Best Local Author Category 2021; and 2021 Readers' Favorite International Book Awards: Gold Medal in the Fiction — Holiday category.

Currently residing in Hamilton, Ontario Canada, she lives with her two sons. She began her writing career after the tragic loss of her parents and husband. Redirecting her emotions through the jotting down of stories became therapeutic in her battle with depression and in 2014 she decided to begin publishing some of her works.

You can sign up for C.A. King's newsletter:
   https://www.subscribepage.com/r8o8y3

Manufactured by Amazon.ca
Bolton, ON